Lost Mage

an Advent Mage novel

Honor Raconteur

 Raconteur House

Published by Raconteur House
Manchester, TN

This is a work of fiction. Names, characters, places and incidents either are the product of the author's imagination or are used ficti-tiously, and any resemblance to actual persons, living or dead, business establishments, events or locales is entirely coincidental.

LOST MAGE

A Raconteur House book/ published by arrangement with the author

PRINTING HISTORY
Raconteur House mass-market edition/November 2014

Copyright © 2014 by Honor Raconteur
Cover design by Honor Raconteur

For information address:
Raconteur House
164 Whispering Winds Dr.
Manchester, TN, 37355

www.raconteurhouse.com

Foreword

The reader should be forewarned that this book is part of a series. In fact, it is a spin-off book of the *Advent Mage Cycle*. The events and characters of this story are directly connected to the original series. It is highly suggested that you read the first four books, starting with *Jaunten*, before reading this one. (Reading the other side novel, *The Dragon's Mage*, is not necessary but encouraged.)

*To all my fans that so patiently
waited for two whole years,
politely nagging for this story. Wish granted!
Also to Dave, our real-life Shad, for inspiring the
character to begin with.*

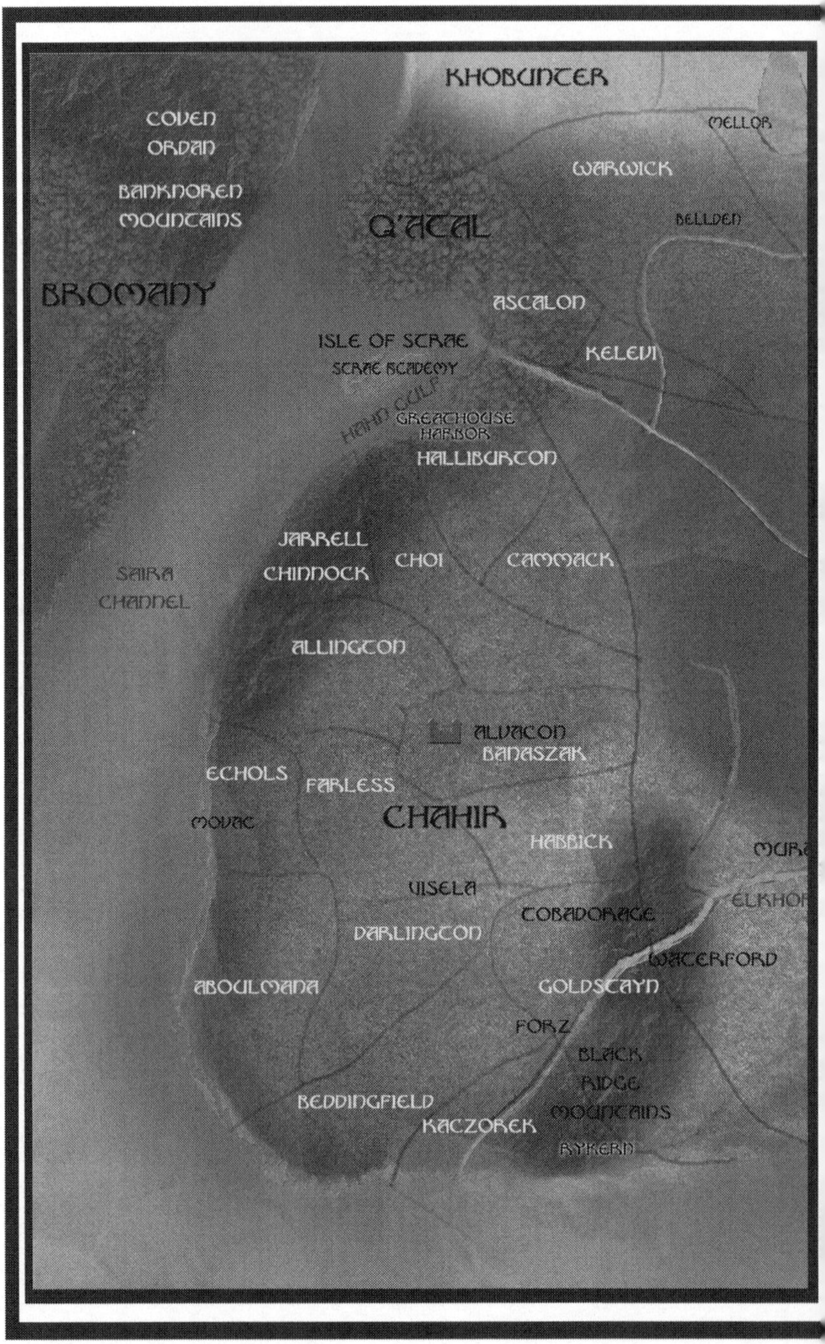
KHOBUNTER
COVEN
ORDAN
MELLOR
WARWICK
BANKNOREN
MOUNTAINS
Q'ATAL
BELLDEN
BROMANY
ASCALON
ISLE OF SCRAE
SCRAE ACADEMY
KELEVI
HAHN GULF
GREATHOUSE
HARBOR
HALLIBURTON
JARRELL
CHOI
CAMMACK
SAIRA
CHANNEL
CHINNOCK
ALLINGTON
ALVACON
BANASZAK
ECHOLS
FARLESS
MOVAC
CHAHIR
HABBICK
VISELA
TOBADORAGE
DARLINGTON
WATERFORD
ABOULMANA
GOLDSTAYN
FORZ
BLACK
RIDGE
MOUNTAINS
BEDDINGFIELD
KACZOREK
RYKERN

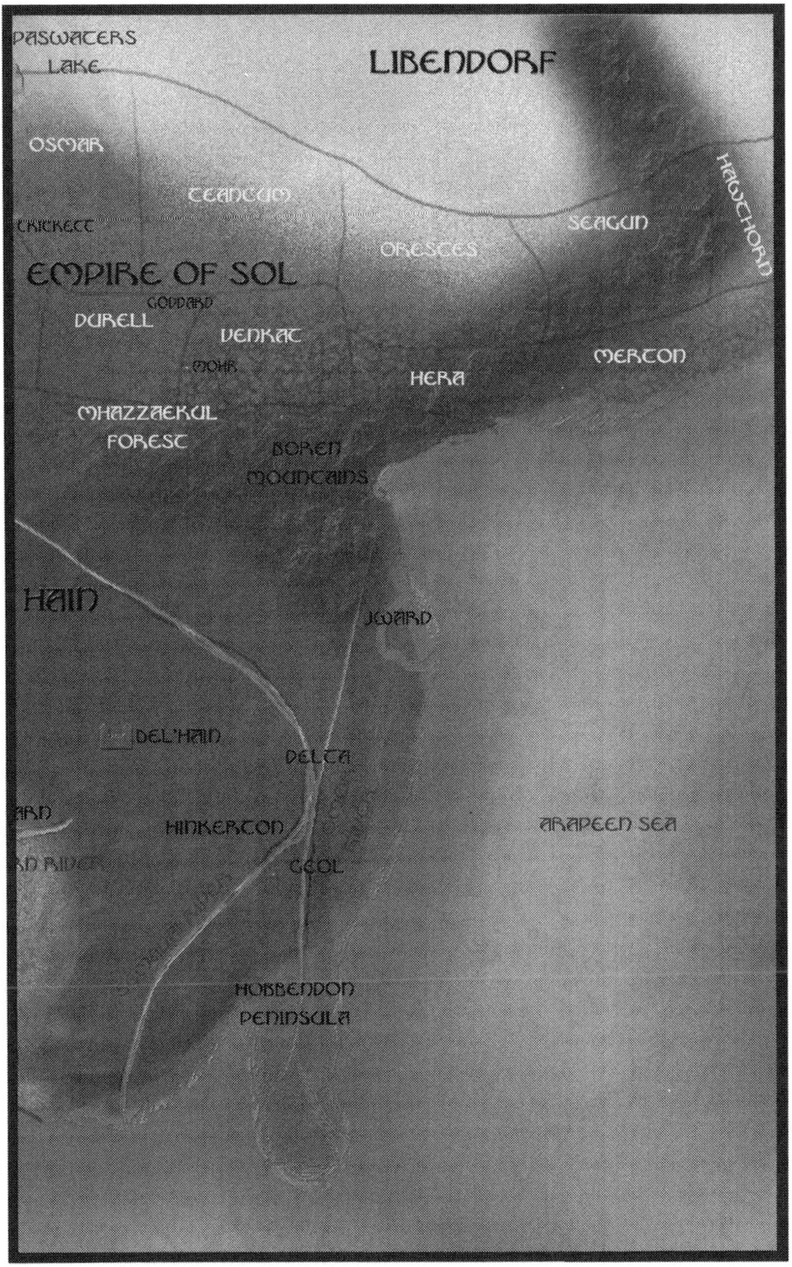
LAKE
LIBENDORF
OSMAR
TEANCUM
SEAGUN
HAWTHORN
ORESTES
EMPIRE OF SOL
GODDARD
DURELL
VENKAT
MOHR
HERA
MERTON
MHAZZAEKUL
FOREST
BOREN
MOUNTAINS
HAIN
JWARD
DEL'HAIN
DELTA
HINKERTON
ARAPEEN SEA
TEOL
HOBBENDON
PENINSULA

Wherever you go, go with all your heart.
Confucius

I stretched my arms above my head with a sigh and smile as the blood got to pumping. Ahh, what a perfectly clear and bright morning. I hadn't seen a day as pretty as this since I'd come back to Ascalon. Xiaolang had talked me into returning with him after Garth and Chatta's wedding, as he wanted me to keep training recruits up here. That was fun, I had to admit. Beating up raw recruits brought a smile to my face.

It had been a year since Strae Academy was built and running, our mission given to us by King Guin deemed complete, and we all returned home. In my case, I'd been building a life here in Ascalon, working alongside the Red Hand. The people had been accommodating here, and welcoming to me, but it didn't feel like *home*. I found myself longing for Chahir sometimes, but my home country had changed past all recognition so that it felt like as much of a stranger to me as Ascalon did.

The home I longed for no longer existed except in my memory and some history books.

I'd been restless and growing unsatisfied for several months now, but I had no direction on where I should go next or what I should try. Xiaolang had talked to me about it several times, but even his empathy and precognitive abilities hadn't been able to really help. I'd been on the verge of recklessly deciding to go on a long, extended trip when a certain letter arrived yesterday.

Garth had written, asking me to become an instructor at Strae Academy. He apparently needed someone to teach weapons.

The school had only been functioning for a year, and I heard that he was getting more students than he knew what to do with. I'd spent most of the night toying with the idea of taking him up on the offer. Perhaps being around my own countrymen again, working with magicians, would give me that elusive sense of belonging I was missing in my life.

Besides, Garth really did have too much on his hands. If nothing else, I could go help him out in the interim while he looked for a more permanent man for the job. Although I wasn't sure if I went and took up the post, he'd ever let me go again. Hmm, decisions, decisions.

I was an active thinker. When I debated something, I tended to go for a run. Part of it was to get blood to my brain so I could think better. But the real benefit was that no one could keep up with me long enough to distract me. So I pulled on a pair of worn-in boots and a thick sweater against the morning chill, before locking up my apartment and leaving.

Several people greeted me as I passed them on the street, but I just waved back without trying to speak and kept up my jog. Once I passed Ascalon's outer wall, I broke into a full run, feeling my muscles warm and loosen as I fell into the right rhythm.

It felt good out here, with the wind in my face and the smell of sunshine and grass wafting around me. I really should come here, outside of the city, to run more often. There were a few farm houses and barns on either side of the road where I ran, but no one was paying attention to me, as they were focused on morning chores. I passed the outer rim of farms and kept going into the open and empty fields.

Only then did I slow down to a walk, breathing hard and wiping sweat from my forehead. I felt better for the run. Now, time to do some serious thinking. What to do about Garth's offer? I was inclined to go just because it was a friend asking for help, and he desperately needed it. But there was a part of me, too, that wanted to invest in Chahir's future. Two hundred years ago, I'd fought to protect the magical community and nearly lost my life in the process. For the past year and a half, I'd fought again to protect it, and this time succeeded. As much as I could within the parameters of the mission, anyway.

If I joined Garth and Chatta at Strae, became an instructor, I could protect the future generations of Chahiran magicians in an entirely different way. I could give them the skills to protect themselves, and wasn't that a better way of doing it? Rather than me running around like a madman trying to protect them all myself?

I'd sorely miss Aletha. I'd miss all the Red Hand, no mistake, but I'd really miss her more than anyone else. We'd been dinner companions and sparring buddies ever since I'd moved up here. What would I do with myself off-duty without her to pester and play with?

That was the only con that I could think of, though. And the benefits outweighed the cons by quite a bit. My selfishness to keep a friend close didn't outweigh everything else. Besides, by going, wouldn't I have Garth and Chatta to play with?

I snorted at myself, amused. Asking myself all these questions was pointless. It sounded like I was rationalizing my decision to go to Strae. I'd already made the decision at some point. Whelp, that was settled, then. I clapped my hands together, satisfied, and turned around to return to Ascalon.

Now, how to break this to Xiaolang.... Urk.

Freezing in midstep, I stared in disbelief. There, standing very calmly in front of me, was a Gardener. Ummm...why did I have a Gardener in front of me? Didn't they normally only want to talk to Garth? And where was the Gardener Expert, anyway, when I needed him?

He approached me on silent feet, the grass not making a sound as it touched him. No wonder I hadn't heard his advance. He moved like he was the wind itself. This Gardener didn't look like either of the ones I'd met before, although, granted, they all looked very similar to each other. He stood as tall as an eight-year-old boy, skin pale like marble, with fine feathers trailing out from his head and cascading to his shoulders. He wore simple clothing of woven material draped over one shoulder, with a belted pouch around his waist.

Obviously, he wanted to talk to me. I'd never seen nor heard of a Gardener making a mistake before. *Why* he wanted to talk to me was a complete mystery, though. I wasn't a magician, and aside from the Jaunten blood Night had given me, I didn't have an ounce of magical ability in me. Copying what I'd seen Garth do, I slowly sank to one knee and held out a hand.

He smiled at me, a small curving of the lips, and took my outstretched hand with warm fingertips.

"*Riicshaden,*" he hailed in a surprisingly deep and clear voice, "*I greet you.*"

"Well met," I responded shakily. Busted buckets, his voice and presence in my head was overwhelming. How had Garth done this? And several times, to boot!

"*We have a task for you.*"

"Ahhh..." It was probably stupid, but I felt compelled to ask anyway. "You sure you want me? Not Garth?"

"*We have a task for you,*" he repeated patiently, a twinkle in his eye. "*A young Weather Mage has awakened in Chahir.*"

A thrill of pure joy and relief shot through me. A Weather Mage. A Weather Mage! YES! I'd feared I'd never hear that another would live.

"*You are relieved to hear this.*"

"I am," I admitted, probably uselessly, as he could

feel everything I felt. "Chahir just doesn't look right to me."

"The land is not as it should be. We awakened a mage and have given her the task of restoring the land."

Wh…what did he just say? They'd *awakened* mage powers in her? So they really had that ability?! Busted buckets, wait until I told Garth that.

"Wait, you said 'her.' The new Weather Mage is a girl?"

"Yes. She is lost. We task you, Riicshaden. You must find her. You must protect her. She is very precious, and if she dies, there will not be another to replace her." With the words came flashes of images that showed me what she looked like, the landscape that she was in, and a disturbing danger that was near her even now.

I swallowed hard. "I understand. I'll leave now."

His eyes crinkled up in a satisfied smile. He leaned forward just enough to pat my arm, as if in gratitude, before he withdrew his hand. Then he turned and walked calmly away.

Now, I was watching carefully. Very, very carefully. But still, within four steps, he'd disappeared into thin air as if he was never there to begin with. How in blue blazes had he done that?

I shook it off and rose to my feet, stretching out my legs so that I could run at full speed back to Ascalon. He hadn't given me a lot of details, but I knew that trouble was brewing, trouble that a young girl couldn't possibly handle by herself. I had to get to her, and as quickly as I could.

But first, I had to contact Garth.

I ran straight to Xiaolang and Asla's home, as Asla was the only witch in the entire city that could use a mirror broach. People watched me sprinting through the city streets like a madman and called out questions of concern after me. I waved a hand, acknowledging them, but didn't slow down enough to offer any reassurances. It was too complex to explain, and I didn't have the time to talk to every single person in this city anyway.

Fortunately for me, Asla and Xiaolang lived not far from the main gates and it didn't take me long to get to their door. I skidded to a halt in front of their low white gate, sweat pouring at my temples and down my back, dragging in air desperately. I might have run here a bit too fast. Ah well.

Asla was working in their front yard, bent near the small garden she kept, her hands efficiently harvesting vegetables and putting them into the basket at her feet. When I roughly pushed the front gate open, she looked up in surprise, eyes wide. "Shad!"

"Asla, I need to talk to Garth," I panted out. "*Now.*"

Her brows furrowed in confusion, but she sensed the urgency and waved me inside. I followed her through the door and to the front room. I had to dodge toys as I went, as they had two small children in the house and a third on the way. Asla navigated her way across the wooden floor with the ease of long practice. She went directly to the mantle above the brick fireplace and touched the mirror hanging there.

"Garth," she called clearly. "Garth, answer me."

Some rustling sounds and muttering came through the mirror before Garth responded, "*Asla, I'm on the way to class.*"

"Shad needs to speak to you. It's urgent."

"*How urgent is urgent?*" Garth said, sounding alarmed.

It was at this point that I irreverently regretted that you couldn't see people through a mirror. Garth's expression was sure to be classic. I came up to stand at Asla's side as I responded, "Garth, I was just given a task by a Gardener."

Several heavy thuds were heard, like he'd just dropped a stack of books. "*You WHAT?!*"

"I don't have time to repeat myself. A Gardener came looking for me this morning and gave me a task. He said there's a young mage that just awakened in southern Chahir. He's tasked me with finding her and protecting her. Garth, I have to get there with all speed. There's a danger hovering over the girl and she's too young to face it alone."

"*How old? Did the Gardener tell you?*"

"I don't know the exact age. He gave me an image of her. She looks like she's about eight or nine."

"*That's very young. And southern Chahir is the*

most dangerous area for budding magicians right now. Shrieking hinges, I don't like the sound of this. Alright, sit tight. I'll come get you and bring you into Chahir myself. Where do I need to take you?"

"I don't *know*," I growled in frustration. "He showed me where she is, but I didn't recognize the place. I wish he'd told me her location...wait, do Gardeners identify places with names?"

"No, human names are completely nonsensical to them. They call us by name as a kindness to us, because they know we'd be completely confused otherwise. He probably gave you all the information he could."

Curses, I was afraid he'd say that. "Alright, from what he showed me, I'd guess it's somewhere south of Darlington Province."

"I'll plan to take you to Darlington, then."

Doing that would take several hours by Earth Path, but it beat spending several weeks on the road to get down there. "I'll pack while I'm waiting for you."

"Be there in an hour," he promised before abruptly cutting the connection.

Asla stood wide-eyed at my side. "Now I understand why you're so frantic. A mage? Do you know what kind?"

At least I would get to enjoy *her* shocked expression. "Weather Mage."

Her jaw dropped, eyes flaring wide. "I thought that line had completely died out!"

"Here's the fun part," I answered with a shaky grin. "It had."

"What?" Her head jerked, surprised and confused.

"What the Gardener said, and I misquote, is that 'we awakened a mage.' So the line was dead, but they found the potential in a girl for mage ability or something, and awakened it in her. He did warn me, though, that if she's lost, there won't be another to replace her."

"They can *awaken* mage abilities," she breathed, looking as shaken by this idea as I felt. "Then...all the mages now..."

"Are likely ones awakened by them, yes, I'll think about that later when I have time." Right now I had precious little time to stand around and chat. "Asla, where's your husband? His office or the training grounds, do you know?"

"Office, I think he said."

I'd try there first. I had to report what was going on before I threw a pack together. Besides, if I was lucky, I might be able to borrow someone to go with me. Going into southern Chahir alone on a rescue mission sounded like an astoundingly bad idea. Oh, it also sounded fun, don't get me wrong. The potential danger sent adrenaline spiking up my spine. But I didn't dare take this mission just for the thrills, like I normally would've. Too much was at stake. I patted Asla on the shoulder in thanks before spinning on my heels and racing out the door.

Ascalon routinely tried to keep its civilian buildings separate from the military compounds and training fields, so getting to Xiaolang wasn't a simple matter of crossing the street. Still, his office was relatively close by, so all it took was for me to go through a checkpoint at the gate and turn a corner to get to the right building. People looked at me askance as I barged through the door and up a short flight of stairs to his office, as I wasn't in uniform like normal, but no one tried to flag me down and talk to me.

Asla turned out to be right and I did find Xiaolang in his office. Thank all the gods above for that small favor as I didn't want to have to hunt the man down. Also fortunately for me, it wasn't just Xiaolang, but Aletha and Eagle there, which increased my chances of being able to borrow someone. They all looked up as I burst through the door.

Xiaolang, no doubt because of his empathy, took only one look at me before he shot out of his chair. "What? What's wrong?"

"Well, it's actually right, with a little wrong mixed in," I corrected.

"Shad!" he groaned. "This is no time for your teasing!"

"What?" Aletha demanded of her captain. "What are you sensing from him?"

"He's emitting urgency like a bonfire on a dark night," Xiaolang explained rapidly. "Shad, *what* is wrong?"

I explained as concisely as I could, for once not taking advantage of the situation and ribbing people any. They listened with growing disbelief, jaws dropping in near-unison. I finished hopefully, "Can I borrow Gorgeous?"

Xiaolang's eyes closed in a pained manner.

"You're going into southern Chahir on a rescue mission to bring back the last possible Weather Mage, and you want just *one* person?"

"I promise to bring her back in one piece," I promised faithfully, hand over my heart.

"Shad, be serious!" Eagle protested. "This isn't a two-man mission. I'm not sure if it's even a two-*squad* mission!"

I dropped into a more somber expression. "Right now I need speed, not manpower. If I can get to the girl fast enough, I can take her away before anyone realizes what she is. That's the impression I got from the Gardener. I don't feel like I should go in there alone, without any backup whatsoever, but more than two people will attract unwanted attention."

As the two men thought that over, I spun on one heel and went down to a knee, taking Aletha's hand in one of mine and looking up with star-struck eyes. "Gorgeous, my dearest, will you be my wife, to have and to hold, for the duration of this mission?"

Not missing a beat, she put a hand to her heart and exclaimed, "Why, Shad, I thought you'd *never* ask me! Of course I will."

Xiaolang looked about two seconds away from banging his head against the desk. Repeatedly. "Shad. Your undercover story is to be a married couple traveling through Chahir?"

I shrugged agreement, bouncing back up to my feet. "If we can pretend to be a married couple on the way out of Chahir, we'll avoid a lot of trouble."

"He's right," Aletha admitted.

"And do you even have anyone else to spare?" I asked Xiaolang, almost rhetorically, as I already knew the answer. "You're due for another mission near the Q'atalian coastline tomorrow, aren't you? You're having to borrow people from another team just to cover everything."

Xiaolang started pacing the length of his office in agitation. "Is Garth going with you?"

"He's on his way now to get me," I answered, carefully omitting the fact that Garth wouldn't be able to join in either. He had a whole academy of students that needed his attention.

"Well, that makes me feel a little better about all of this..." Xiaolang trailed off in a mutter. "Alright, fine. So, pretend to be a married couple, eh?" He had that empaths-are-scary smile he sometimes wore as he looked at the two of us.

I blinked and shared a look with Aletha, but she clearly didn't understand why Xiaolang would look at us like that either.

"Something you want to share with us, Captain?" she asked him with mounting suspicion.

"No," he denied, smile widening. "You'll figure it out, between the two of you. Aletha, go with him."

I think she wanted to sit on Xiaolang until she strangled some answers from his cryptic little neck, but she thought better of it and simply nodded in agreement before turning to me. "How much time do I have to pack?"

"Garth said he would come to get me in about an hour, and that was a good twenty minutes ago."

"So, five minutes to pack." She didn't look particularly disturbed by this. A veteran soldier, she knew how to prepare in a hurry. With a salute to Xiaolang, she exited the office quickly.

With a gamine grin, I waved at the two men. "Wish us luck!"

"Just don't get killed?" Xiaolang pleaded. "I don't want to have to do the paperwork for it."

Some friend he was. Laughing, I shrugged the concern away before following after Aletha.

We waited outside the city gates for Garth, as he tended to cause mass panic in the streets when he popped up in the city. Aletha and I both had our horses with us, packs on their backs, and the clothes that we'd worn while on our missions in Chahir. We'd still attract attention—mostly because of Aletha's dark hair and olive skin—but since I was obviously Chahiran, hopefully people would buy the 'we're married' story and not give us trouble.

Well, maybe. I did a mental evaluation of my appearance, frowning thoughtfully as I realized I didn't look purely Chahiran anymore. My skin was a swarthy tan after spending so much time outdoors training people. My hair had become pure white after being turned Jaunten, making me look a decade older than I actually was. After so many years of serving in various militaries, I had the bearing of a soldier stamped into me. Would my countrymen look at me and automatically assume I was one of them? Now there was the question.

I glanced at Aletha. Beautiful and exotic-looking as always. Being a natural infiltration specialist, she had changed out of the black and red Ascalon uniform and into clothes that would blend in better with Chahir's fashions. She knew enough Chahirese to get by, but she would never be confused for a native. Not with her obviously Solian looks and military bearing. No, it might be better for both of us to stay out of sight as much as possible.

The ground melted to either side not five feet in front of us, and Garth slowly rose to the surface. He still had on the dark brown robes of a professor, so he obviously hadn't bothered to change before coming to get us. I silently blessed his speed, as we needed it.

"Ready?" he asked, already walking closer to us.

"Yes," Aletha answered, expression strained. Oh, right, she hated traveling by Earth Path. I'd forgotten that.

"Then let's go." So saying, he whirled the earth around us like it was nothing more than putty in a sculptor's hands, bringing us down into the earth itself. It was dark, smelled slightly dank, and the walls glowed with magic. Just like the last dozen times I'd been down here. I'd never in a million years understand why Garth liked it underground.

I glanced at Aletha. She looked pale, as if the blood had just drained out of her face, and her eyes were screwed shut. I felt a twinge of sympathy for her. Part of me thought I shouldn't have brought her along since she hated earth-traveling so much, but really, she was the best person to bring in this situation and I couldn't regret it.

Hoping to offer a little comfort, I grabbed her hand and squeezed it. Her hand closed around mine and she held on as if I were a lifeline.

Garth looked down, noticed our linked hands, then his eyes took in Aletha's face. "Ahhh, right, you don't like it down here."

"Hurry," Aletha requested in a thin voice. "Please."

"I'm going as fast as I can," he assured her.

I reexamined Aletha's expression. Despite the death grip she had on my hand, she still looked almost unbearably terrified to be down here. I didn't share her fear of underground spaces like this, but I could relate, after spending two hundred years in a space so confining I couldn't even twitch a muscle. Having sympathy for her, I put my free arm around her shoulders and pulled her into my side.

She slit open one eye to look up at me askance. "Yes?"

"Aren't you supposed to take advantage of situations like this?" I responded, lips kicked up on one side. "What do you think husbands are for, anyway?"

"An excellent point," she agreed before latching her arms around my waist. The grip was bruisingly tight, although she left me enough room to breathe.

"Ahhh…" Garth trailed off, staring at us with a dumbfounded expression. "Husband?"

I had my mouth open, ready to take him for a ride, when Aletha beat me to it by explaining, "We're playing the part of a couple on this mission."

His suspicions immediately disappeared. "Oh, I see."

"Spoilsport," I muttered to her, making a face.

"Behave, hubby dearest. You have a lot of important information to give to Garth before he drops us off. We can't afford for you to go off on one of your teasing tangents."

She was unfortunately right. I turned back to him. "Can I talk to you as you go?" Sometimes Garth could handle conversations while he navigated. There were times he couldn't, though. It depended on how well he knew the area.

"Yes," he assured me. "Tell me in detail what the Gardener said."

"Before I do that, brace yourself," I requested cheerfully.

Garth's eyes cut sideways. "That smile you're wearing is scaring me. Shad. What did you forget to mention to me?"

"Forget?" I responded, putting a wounded hand over my heart. "Nonsense. I just wanted to see your reaction in person."

His eyes narrowed, tone growling in warning, "Shad."

He was sooo fun to tease. "I mentioned I'm going after a mage. Guess what kind."

It took him a second, then his lips parted in wonder. "Don't tell me. A Weather Mage?"

"You're quick," I approved.

Garth's expression was a mix of delight and nervousness, as if he couldn't decide whether to be glad that a whole line of magic hadn't died out or not. Then again, it would be *his* job to train the new mage, and no one in the world could help him. No one really had remembered there were Weather Mages until I'd reminded them.

Swallowing hard, he choked out, "You're sure?"

"Oh, quite sure."

Aletha grabbed a good inch of flesh around my ribs and gave me the mother of all pinches. "Ouch! What was that for?"

"Shad," Aletha requested mildly, "start from the beginning and tell us everything."

"Use your words, wifey, violence is unbecoming. OWW! Fine, fine, stop pinching me."

I faithfully retold the story, trying to be as close to verbatim as possible. They listened attentively, without interrupting, until I finished.

"He actually said that they'd *awakened* a mage," Garth repeated, voice shaken.

"That was the word he used," I confirmed. "Which means that the theory you had about the Gardeners directly interfering with the magic in Chahir was dead-on."

Garth let out a low whistle. "I'm glad to have that confirmed, though. Before, it was just a gut feeling. But it's obvious, too, that the Coven Ordan magicians, Aral especially, was right in their theories. They thought it took a certain talent to be a magician, that you had to have the predisposition for it, in order for your magic to awaken. What the Gardener said makes me think they were right. Otherwise, if it was solely

up to them, then they could awaken as many Weather
Mages as they wished to."

True. "I wonder why they're doing it now. I mean,
isn't she too young for mage abilities?"

"I'm still wondering why they awakened Nolan
and Trev'nor when they did," Garth responded with a
brief frown. "They were even younger."

Oh, right. They had been, at that. "Any chance
they'd explain that to us?"

Garth gave me a look that spoke volumes.

I let out a sigh. "Right, I didn't think they would.
Just a hope on my part."

"But wouldn't it have been better to send us
to fetch the girl *before* they awakened her magic?"
Aletha looked a little strange participating in this conversation with her eyes screwed shut like that. I had to
bite my lip to keep from laughing at her.

"I'm assuming they had good reason to do what
they did," Garth responded with a shrug. "They always
do. It might have been a simple matter of timing. She
was in the right area of the country to be influenced by
the power of the ley lines around her, so they had to
awaken her then. Or it could've been that they knew
no parent would give her up unless her magic was
active, so in order for us to take her out of Chahir,
she had to be a mage first. I'm offering purely human
theories, mind. I have no idea what they were thinking
when they did it."

Yes, that was the fun part about dealing with the
Gardeners. They rarely gave you an explanation of
what was going on. We typically got just enough infor-

mation to work with before they disappeared.

Garth caught my eye. "When you do find her, head directly east and get out of Chahir. Don't try to travel through it. Chatta's notifying King Guin right now and sending magicians to the old safe houses. They'll help relay you to the Isle of Strae."

Sound advice, and more or less what I'd already been planning to do. Vonlorisen had ordered his people to disband the Star Order and accept magic again, but a two-hundred-year-old prejudice was not so easily abolished. I had no intention of staying in Chahir any longer than we needed to.

"But don't stray too far into Hain, either," Garth cautioned, an odd note of frustration in his tone. "I'm still struggling with the Trasdee Evondit Orra when it comes to the mages. The witches and wizards born in Chahir they won't fight me over, but since the only mages born are in Chahir, they seem to think that they can have half of them."

I blinked, incredulous. "That's...."

"Ridiculous?" he finished sourly. "Tell me about it. Even now, they think of mages as some sort of commodity more than anything else. I've even argued this point with O'danne and Doss. I did ask Guin covertly for help, but if they get wind of an awakened Weather Mage, I'll have a full-blown fight on my hands. We *must* get her to Strae before they find out about her; otherwise we might lose her to Hain."

"We can't!" I objected. "The Gardeners awakened her for Chahir's benefit, not Hain's."

"I know. Which is why you have to be careful. I

wish I could stay, help you find her," Garth fretted, brows furrowed. "But I don't dare leave a handful of instructors up there with a school full of students. We're just barely managing as it is, and they can't afford for me to go off for several days."

"I know," I assured him. "I never expected you to stay. Besides, if the situation needed you, then I'm sure a Gardener would have come to see you too. But I'm the one they asked, so I must be sufficient."

He nodded with a long, resigned sigh. "That's the only thing that makes me feel better about all of this. They never give anyone a task they can't manage. I suppose while you're busying finding the girl, we'll go through the archives and figure out how to train her."

As the only living Weather Mage, she'd be forced to learn from books and conjecture instead of real-life instruction. Poor kid. But Garth had done the same thing and came through it fine, so hopefully she wouldn't accidentally destroy the world while she figured things out.

"Garth, one more thing." I waited until he looked at me before saying, "I meant to say this before I got the surprise visit, but I'll take the position you offered as Weapons Professor."

Aletha jerked in surprise, her eyes snapping open. "What?!"

"You will?" A grin stretched over his face from ear to ear. "Phew, I'm glad! You're really the best fit for the job. I couldn't think of whom else to ask."

"I wanted to, but it turns out I'll need to anyway." I looked at Aletha out of the corner of my eye as I said this. I probably should have said something to Xiaolang and the rest before telling Garth, but I'd had no time for a debate before, and they would have demanded explanations after I'd more or less set up a life in Ascalon. "When the Gardener said 'go protect her,' he didn't mean short-term. I *felt* it when he said it. He meant for a lifetime. I can't leave her alone once I find her."

Aletha's hands clenched my shirt. "I understand that she's precious, irreplaceable, and has to be safe-guarded, but...a lifetime?"

"I wouldn't choose anyone else to protect her," Garth said frankly. "Then, you'll take the position and stay throughout her schooling?"

"At least," I agreed. "After that, who knows? It depends on what she needs to do."

Aletha dragged a hand roughly over her face. "How is it that you never take the easy road? Every time, you take on the impossible tasks, the ones that no man really wants to do."

"Now, Gorgeous," I chided with open amusement, "where would the fun be in taking the easy way?"

To Garth, she groaned, "I can't figure out who's crazier. Him or me for following him."

He just shook his head, eyes twinkling. "And to think, I'm the one that set him loose on the world again."

"Oh, that's true." She snapped her fingers, as if only now remembering this. "I can blame you for let-ting him out of the crystal if anything goes wrong."

"It's all the better if you have a scapegoat handy,"

I agreed, trying not to laugh.

"That said, try to keep a low profile?" Garth re-quested of us both. "I can't give you a mirror broach or any way to contact us if something goes wrong. You're truly on your own down here."

I dismissed this with an airy wave. "We'll be fine."

Garth dropped us well out of the sight of a de-cent-sized village on the border of Darlington and Far-less Province. I could tell he wanted to stay and help, but almost before we could rise above ground, Chatta contacted him by mirror with a problem that involved a gaping hole in the wall. How a student had acciden-tally destroyed part of the academy already, I didn't know, but from the way that Garth failed to react to this news, I figured it wasn't the first time something like this had happened. Just how dangerous was it, anyway, teaching people to use magic? I'd thought it would be a fairly tame job, but it just might keep me on my toes.

He left in a hurry, and so did we. Aletha and I had packed for this trip, but we hadn't gone shopping for the necessary food supplies before Garth came for us. We'd put that off for a reason. We needed information as much as food for the road, and it was best to get both at the same time.

With that in mind, we entered the town of Visela.

We came in at a trot but had to slow the pace once we came to the main road that bisected the town. There was enough foot traffic, street vendors, and carts to make the road somewhat difficult to navigate. I looked around with interest as we entered. This seemed to be something of a trading town, as I saw signs of all different types of merchants and wares out for sale. I also heard different dialects being spoken, ranging from a Jarrellan accent to a Kaczorekan one. I doubted that Aletha could tell the difference—she hadn't used any of her Chahirese since we'd stopped searching in this country almost a year ago. She was sure to be rusty and out of practice by now.

She pulled her gelding in tighter to me so that she could speak without shouting over the din. "I don't think we're going to find a lot of information here."

"You might be surprised," I responded. I had to pause while speaking to dodge a loaded wagon that had stopped right in the middle of the road. When I came around it and back to Aletha's side, I continued, "I'm hearing accents from all provinces, especially from the far southern side of the country."

"Oh?" she perked up, much more alert. "In that case, you want to split up? Say, you get the breads, cheeses, and meats, I'll get everything else? We're more likely to get information that way."

I took another look around us, twisting this way and that in the saddle. I saw quite a few dark heads mixed into the crowd. There might be enough foreigners here that Aletha wouldn't really warrant a second glance. "You don't think you'll be hassled?"

She arched an eyebrow at me, head slanted in a challenging manner. "You think it would matter?"

"Yes, wifey, I'm aware that you can beat a lecher's face flat, that's not what I'm saying," I drawled patiently. "We *are* supposed to keep things low-key, remember?"

"I promise to beat them up silently," she retorted sweetly.

Why was I even worrying about her? It was the possible lechers that needed my sympathy. "Fine, fine. Then, meet me there," I jerked my chin to indicate the fountain that sat in the middle of the town square, "in an hour?"

"That should be enough time," she judged. "Then, in an hour."

The market made a split and our noses basically told us which directions we needed to go. I followed the smell of baking bread to the left, and Aletha spied vegetables farther up the street and kept going. I discovered quickly that I couldn't keep riding, or even lead my stallion along, as the market started crowding over the street. It became close quarters, so tight that I myself had to go sideways just to make it through.

I found a carriage house around the corner that agreed to hold my horse for a small fee, and I left what I'd already bought with the stallion. Then I went back to the street, haggling for bread and cheese and jerky. I asked questions of the merchants and vendors as I went, looking for anything strange that might be weather-related, but no one had heard of anything. In fact, I got odd looks for even asking, as apparently the weather this season was unusually fair.

This relieved me in a sense, because it meant that the girl mage hadn't been discovered yet, but it also meant that I didn't have any indicators of where to go except in a southerly direction.

That was less than helpful.

It was instinct that made me turn a corner, stealing a glance behind me as I did so. I saw them instantly. Three men, armed with knives and long walking sticks that could be quarterstaffs if needed. They looked rough, their clothes shoddy, beards and hair ill-kept, and I fancied that even from this distance I could smell the cheap alcohol on them. Street thieves, and hardened ones, from the looks of it.

Growling to myself, I started looking for a place to lose them. I didn't need to tangle with the city guard. Way too many questions would be involved and the answers could tie me up for weeks. It would be better all-around if I could just ditch them here and bypass all that trouble.

My eyes nearly skipped over it, the opening was so narrow. It was a dinky little alleyway, probably only used for refuse, crammed in between two buildings. Perfect. I ducked in between two food stalls, blocking the vision of my would-be-thieves, and then dove into the alleyway. There were several crates stacked up on one side and I scrambled behind them, sinking down to one knee to keep my head out of view.

The smell of the alleyway wasn't exactly pleasant—actually, it stank to high heaven. It was like leather armor not cleaned in three months, dead fish left out for a few days, and Chatta's potions all mixed into one. I nearly gagged. To keep my mind off of it, I strained my hearing to the max, trying to figure out if I had lost my tagalongs or not.

I didn't hear them...of course, with all the city sounds out there, I probably wouldn't...*yeeooooow-ww!*

From out of nowhere a striped orange and white cat had appeared and taken a layer of skin off my hand. With an angry hiss, it arched its back, hair standing on end, and snarled at me. Cripes, was I intruding on its territory?

"Just put up with me for a bit, would ya?" I pleaded in a soft whisper. "I'll be out of your furballs in a minute."

He didn't like this answer and took another swipe at me. I avoided this one in the nick of time, and I decided that since negotiations had obviously failed, I was going to have to go with more drastic measures. Reaching for him quickly, I tried to snatch the alley cat up by the back of the neck.

Being a fast little bugger, he dodged and landed another hit on me.

Swearing, I reached for him again, just catching him by the front leg. He promptly leaned over and bit me, levering up all his paws so that he could dig in with three sets of claws. Hissing in pain—that bloody well *hurt!*—I clamped my free hand over his mouth to stifle the angry, screeched challenges he was making.

Of all the blasted luck! Why did I have to dive into the one alleyway in all of Visela that had a territorial alley cat in it?

My tagalongs hadn't heard the commotion and come to investigate, had they? I pressed the cat against my chest, restricting his movements, and cautiously eased one eye around the crates.

Nothing.

No one had heard the cat and me tussling. Or maybe they had heard and dismissed it as nothing of consequence. Whatever the case might've been, no one was even bothering to glance into the alley.

Hoping that I had lost the pursuers, I got to my feet and cautiously made my way to the mouth of the alley. Staying low to the ground, I peeked in either direction. No sign of them anywhere. Blowing out a breath of relief, I turned my attention to my more immediate trouble. The cat was still now, but I was sure that the minute I let go of him, he was going to come right back at me, all claws bared. Maybe if I tossed him farther into the alley and hightailed it out of his territory, he wouldn't pursue me?

Since I couldn't think of another plan, I went with it. Supposedly, if you picked up a cat by the back of their neck, they couldn't move. Or at least Chatta always picked up Didi that way, and Meurittas were rather similar to cats…. Shrugging, I lifted my hand off his mouth and grabbed his neck.

Wait a minute, he wasn't making any noise. I hadn't smothered him, had I? A little worried, I maneuvered him so that I could look at his face. Well, his eyes were closed, but he was still breathing. So he was just unconscious? Good then, I could just put him down—hold it.

Out of the corner of my eye, I had caught a flicker of movement that seemed odd. Focusing, I looked closer at his front paws. In front of my disbelieving eyes, his fur was slowly losing its stripes, turning a uniform white.

Shrieking hinges!

I didn't see how it was possible, I couldn't imagine how it was working, but the evidence was in front of my eyes and I couldn't refute it. Somehow, I had accidentally turned this cat Jaunten.

A *cat* as a *Jaunten.*

Never in my life did I wish that I had either Garth or Chatta nearby so badly. I needed someone to explain this to me. As far as I knew—and I was Jaunten, so I should've known *something,* right?!—this wasn't even possible. Sure, Night was Jaunten, which was very unusual. But even though a Nreesce was in the body of a horse, it was still a sentient creature. It had always been assumed that it was only because of Night's intelligence that the Jaunten blood had taken hold.

Last I'd checked, cats weren't known to talk much or think like humans.

I shook my head to clear it from going around in dizzy circles. I couldn't just stand here until I figured this out. At the rate I was going, that'd take a few decades. I made a snap decision to just take the cat with me. I could figure this out later, once I was safely out of the city and away from any curious eyes.

First I had to figure out how to tell Aletha.

I'd pulled a lot of stupid, crazy stunts in my life. Because of that, I'd gotten some pretty interesting looks from people, but I do believe that Aletha's expression took the prize. She gave me the blankest, most dumbfounded look I'd ever seen on a person's face. Her mouth kept moving, too, like she wanted to say something only couldn't find the words.

"You...turned a cat...Jaunten," she said slowly, as if she were trying to use those words to do some sort of complicated mathematical problem, only it wasn't adding up.

"I think he's about half-baked," I responded with a deliberately devil-may-care grin. Holding up the cat by the scruff of his neck, I pointed at the area that was quickly turning solid white. "See how half of him is still tabby? I give it another hour before we have a fully-turned Jaunten cat on our hands."

"*How* did this happen?" she demanded, pointing accusingly at the cat.

"He bit me!" I retorted defensively.

"No, I mean *how?*"

Oh, she meant 'how' as in, how was this even possible. "That I don't know," I admitted. "According to my Jaunten knowledge, this can't happen. But then, according to my Jaunten knowledge, no one has ever tried this before either. I wonder what other animals this would work with...."

"Shad, focus!" she growled at me. Her eyes darted around, looking to see if anyone was eavesdropping.

Why she bothered, I didn't know, as I had taken the precaution of dragging her out of town before telling her anything. We were at a well near a copse of trees that gave us some shelter and water to fill our canteens with. There was not a blessed soul near us, except for a few people on the road, but they were a good twenty feet away and not within earshot. Still, she lowered her voice even further.

"What are we going to do with him? We can't very well let a cat with Jaunten blood run around southern Chahir."

"We're not even sure at this point how effective the Jaunten blood will be with him," I pointed out. "I say we travel, wait for him to turn, then try to talk to him when he wakes up. At the rate he's going, it won't take much longer."

"Hmm, I suppose that's the only sensible plan to take." Staring at the cat, her mouth pursed. "He's not much to look at, is he?"

No, he truly wasn't. He had a good long split in one ear, as if he'd been in a fight and it had never healed properly. His tail was outright missing, he had

lumps in his fur from where burs had gotten tangled and matted, and he smelled vile.

"Before he wakes up, let's give him a good scrubbing." Aletha picked him out of my hands and laid him on the ground next to the well.

Bathe a sleeping, defenseless cat? Inspired decision. Call me a coward if you must, but I had no desire to wrestle with him again and get *more* scratches to show for it.

I cranked the lever on the well and drew up a bucket of water as Aletha rummaged around in her packs for a bar of soap and a towel. Between the two of us, we scrubbed him from head to toe three times before the smell was gone. Then we dunked him in the bucket several times to get all the soap out of his fur. Aletha even went so far as to comb him out and take a knife to the worst of the clumps.

He looked like a mangy, drowned rat by the time we were through with him.

But at least he smelled better!

After wrapping him up in the towel, we cleaned up and mounted, heading south on the highway. Because of our delay in shopping, and dealing with him, we'd lost more than the hour we'd allotted for our stop and it was now close to midafternoon. I squinted at the sky, estimating that we had perhaps another four hours of daylight left to travel in. Fortunately for us, it was summer and that gave us a lot of light. Of course, it also meant riding became unbearably hot at times, but getting sunburned and sweaty wouldn't kill us.

"Hubby dearest?"

"Yes, darling?"

"What exactly do you plan to do about the Trasdee Evondit Orra when we get back?" Aletha jerked her chin to indicate the sleeping cat curled up in my lap. "You know they'll find out about him one way or another. Aside from breaking two or three laws, you've also set a new magical precedent."

"Which would be the second one," I joked, shrug rueful. "As they're still trying to figure out how I lasted for two hundred years in that crystal."

"That one wasn't your doing," she pointed out calmly. "*This* one is."

"Actually, it isn't," I retaliated sweetly. "As I said, *his* doing."

"Shad. You're the super soldier. You're honestly expecting me to believe that you couldn't dodge an alley cat?"

"The term 'catlike reflexes' exists for a reason, dearest."

She rolled her eyes. "Still doesn't answer my original question. What are you going to say to the Trasdee Evondit Orra?"

"That they do not govern the magic in Chahir, so this is not their problem." I beamed, satisfied with my own answer.

Her look in my direction said she didn't give that plan a very high rate of success. I had to admit, it was a bit weak. But then, what she'd failed to consider was I had an ace up my sleeve.

Eyebrow cocked, her eyes studied my face for a long moment. "You plan to let Garth get you out of this situation, don't you?"

I reeled in my saddle as if shocked. "You can read minds now?!"

She snorted, amused. "Only yours, darling. But then, you're easy to predict."

Most people found me very *un*predictable, actually. I think it was more a matter of her knowing me very well.

I knew the instant that the cat awoke. He went from a peacefully sleeping creature in my lap to a hissing, spitting, half-wet furball in a split second. Before I knew it, he'd somehow wrangled his way out of the towel and leapt for the ground, landing in a sideways slide on the grass.

"Oh, you're awake," I greeted pleasantly, leaning over my stallion's neck to look him in the eye. "Greetings."

He arched his back and hissed at me. The look was somewhat marred since half his fur had dried in a weird direction, so it refused to stand up properly along his spine.

"Now, I'm not going to apologize for the change you went through," my tone was perfectly level, "as you rather brought it upon yourself by biting me. I won't apologize for the bath, either, as you sorely needed it."

I got quite the dirty look for that. I'd always harbored the suspicion that it wasn't water or baths that cats hated, it was just having to put all their fur back in place that irked them.

"We just have two questions for you." Aletha

dropped out of her saddle and stared cautiously at the
cat. The expression on her face said she felt a little silly for seriously conversing with a four-legged creature.
(Why, I didn't know, as it didn't bother me.) "Do you
realize what you are?"

The cat's ears went flat, creating the perfect look
of annoyance. After a long moment he gave a very
human nod.

My mouth went dry. I couldn't mistake that gesture for anything other than assent. Heavens. Wait
until the magic council heard about *this*.

Aletha wet her lips and continued hoarsely, "Can
you understand perfectly everything I'm saying?"

He drew himself up in a dignified way and gave
us such a superior look that it left us no doubt that he
did, in fact, understand. The look made us feel stupid
for even questioning it.

I let out a low whistle. "So that theory of Night
only becoming Jaunten because of his sentient intelligence just went up in smoke. Last I checked, cats
weren't supposed to be that smart."

The cat didn't care for that statement one bit.

Aletha waved me down. "Look, if you have Shad's
knowledge, then you know where we're going and
why. You also realize how dangerous it is for you to
stay in Chahir. If anyone suspects what you are—and
they have ways of detecting the magic in you—then
they'll hunt you down. Killing you will probably be
the kindest thing they do to you. Since that's the case,
won't you go back with us? We can take you to Strae
Academy, which is the safest place for you to be. You

won't lack for anything there, either."

I rather hoped he'd agree, as I enjoyed the thought of showing a Jaunten cat to all those oh-so-masterful magicians and watching their eyes bug out of their heads.

The cat considered us both for a long moment, and I could just see the wheels spinning in his head, but he finally consented with a flick of his ear. Then, to the surprise of us both, he gave a light hop from the ground and settled on my stallion's haunches. I twisted with a creak of leather to look behind me.

"You sure you want to ride there?" I asked in surprise. "You won't fall off?"

He gave me a look that adequately said, *Please. As if I would.*

I held up a hand in surrender. "Alright, fine, sorry I asked. Gorgeous, let's get going."

"Wait, I don't think it's right to just pick up a companion and travel with him without knowing his name," she protested. "I mean, what if we need to call him?"

Good point. Although it begged the question: "Do cats even have names?"

He started licking his paw, completely bored with this conversation.

I'd take that as a "no." Hmmm, in that case...I gave him a thorough scrutiny, trying to think of a name for him. He was a pristine white now, but still looked like a beat-up alley cat. I wasn't going to name him something cute like Snow.

"Tail."

Both cat and woman gave me a funny look, as if my naming sense didn't have any logic to it.

"Because he's tailing us until we reach Strae," I explained. "Besides, he doesn't have one. A tail, I mean. Isn't it perfect?"

Aletha gave a put-upon sigh. "I suppose I shouldn't have expected much since you named your dark bay stallion Cloud. Fine, Tail works. Let's keep riding."

We got some strange looks as we traveled the main highway south, let me tell you. It was common for people to travel with dogs as protection or because they were moving flocks of sheep, that sort of thing. And varieties of farm animals were a regular sight in a company of travelers as well. But a cat? No one traveled with a cat unless it was a fine lady of some sort. And even then, the pampered feline was riding in a carriage on a silk cushion, not lounging on the back of a stallion.

What made the situation stranger, from their perspective at least, was that Aletha and I were carrying on a conversation with him.

It was actually quite fascinating. I started with my earliest piece of knowledge, something I'd inherited from the Jaunten blood, and started asking him questions. Despite the fact that he couldn't speak, he was quite capable of conversing with body language and perfectly-timed meows and sniffs. He knew everything I knew, and he wasn't shy about letting us know it, either.

I had to wonder, if it worked this well on cats, how

would it work on Meurittas?

Then I imagined Didi with a human's intelligence and shuddered. No, some things were better left alone.

We found a small brook off the side of the highway and made camp for the night. Tail proved to be a good fisher, as he caught a small river trout and dragged it over to the fire. Then he dropped it on my boot and gave me a significant look.

I looked back at him blankly. "What?" I doubted he was feeding me.

Aletha looked up from where she was unpacking the cookware. "Shad, I think he expects you to clean that for him."

Tail gave a satisfied purr, happy with her translation.

"Wait, last I checked, cats don't care if a fish is raw or not," I protested.

Aletha and Tail's eyes met and she gave a shrug. "Apparently, turning him Jaunten has given him some human habits."

Just how could she understand him so well? I knew that women and cats were a lot alike, but still.... Resigned to my fate, I picked up the fish and went back to the stream so that I could clean it. I even baked it in the coals for Lord Furball, as he seemed to expect that as well.

With him purring and contentedly eating his fish, Aletha and I managed to cook up a stew and some flatbread for our own dinner. As we ate, Aletha asked, "So what exactly are we looking for?"

"I think it's further south than this," I answered thoughtfully. "The land the Gardener showed me looked like grassland, but it had a lot of low hills and rocks. I got the impression of water too, so maybe near a large lake? Or even the sea, for all I know."

"So you don't think we're even in the right province?"

"No, not really," I admitted. "I had Garth drop us off in Darlington because I didn't want to paint a target on the girl mage's location. That earth-traveling method of his sends off all sorts of magical flares."

"It was probably for the best, but that also means it's going to take us longer to reach her."

I set my bowl down on the ground with a sigh. "It's a fine line to tread, to be sure. I hope I don't regret the decision later."

"Are you sure we shouldn't have kept him around? I mean, he could have felt where she was and taken us directly to her."

I shook my head. "There had to be a reason why the Gardener came to get me instead of Garth. If it was speed needed to rescue her, it would have been him they called for. No, I think we can find her just as well without him. Besides, we were lucky to keep him for as long as we did."

She chuckled in agreement. "Yes, it did seem like a disaster was waiting for him at the academy. How do you suppose a student managed to blow a hole in the building?"

"Who knows? Potions accident, maybe?"

"I never thought that being a teacher at a magical

academy should involve hazard pay until now."

I laughed outright at this. "Maybe I should negotiate for that before signing on, since I'll be teaching weapons."

"I want to meet the kid that can hurt *you*," she retorted, "and recruit him myself!"

"Hey, it's possible!" I protested, still smiling. "Not likely, I'll grant you."

"Pfft." Shaking her head, she put her hands on her knees and pushed herself up to her feet. "I'll get more firewood."

"Alright." I supposed while she did that, I should start cleaning up.

Tail dragged a fish over to me and dropped it at my feet, manner imperious.

I looked at the fish, then looked back at him. "Another one?"

He flicked his ear in affirmation before sitting down like a prim and proper lord.

Heaven spare me. Cats were egotistical creatures to begin with, but give them a little intelligence, and they thought they could rule the universe. Rolling my eyes, I reached for the fish and started cleaning it. I didn't dare do otherwise. Cats could be creative and outright cruel when getting revenge.

If only I could somehow divide up the intelligence. My stallion had good staying power and was well-trained, so he didn't spook easily, but he could be a brighter horse. I called him Cloud because it always seemed like his head was up in the clouds. Even now, standing over there nibbling on the grass, he looked dazed and out of it.

My eyes trailed back to the cat sitting patiently at my side. I'd asked this question before, although Aletha had quickly squashed the idea. If I could turn a cat Jaunten, what other animals would it work on? Really, the first animal I would have chosen to experiment with was a horse, as Jaunten blood worked well with Nreesces.

"You're cleaning and cooking another fish for him?" Aletha asked in amusement, coming around the campfire with some firewood in her hands.

"Oh?" I blinked, switching back to the present. "Uh, yes. I don't dare do otherwise. I don't know what he'll do to me if I don't."

She chuckled. "Yes, cats are good at getting revenge. Tail, you know that I'll cook fish for you too?"

Tail gave her a bored look.

"Apparently I'm a good cook," I drawled, amused when he gave a very human nod of agreement.

"With fish, you are," Aletha agreed, her pride not the least bit singed. But then, my superior fish cooking skills made me Tail's personal chef, so she likely thought she was getting the better end of the deal. "Well, if you're cooking again, I'll get another bucket of water."

"Sure, thanks." I watched her leave the campfire's light and pass into the shadows again. My mind went back to thinking about Cloud. Would it work?

Would it hurt anything to try?

The only con I could foresee was riding around on a white horse. And that was if it worked. If it failed, it wouldn't do anything. Well, except get me into trouble with Aletha, who doubtless wouldn't look well upon my experimenting. But potential trouble had never stopped me from trying anything.

I quickly propped the fish up near the fire so that it would cook, then skirted around to Cloud's side. Before Aletha could come back and stop me, I nicked my wrist with the knife and then nicked him on the neck. Being a good-tempered horse, he just flinched and didn't try to head-butt me. I quickly put my bleeding wrist up against his neck, watching the blood mix together.

With one eye on him, one eye on where Aletha had disappeared into the trees, I held that position for several long seconds. I couldn't see her in the darkness, but I could hear her boots as they slapped against the tall grass, so I didn't have more than a few moments before she came back and asked what in blue blazes I was doing.

At that moment, Cloud's eyes rolled back into his head. With a yelp, I quickly scrambled away before he sank to the ground and onto his side. If I hadn't moved that fast, he would have pinned me underneath him. I scanned him anxiously, looking for signs of him turning white, but didn't see anything yet. Then again, it would likely take longer to work on a horse. Let's see…it took six hours for a human to convert, two for a cat…so perhaps ten or so hours for a horse? If we were just going by body weight.

"Shad."

I spun about with a bright, innocent smile on my

face. "Yes?"

Aletha had both arms crossed over her chest, a hard look in her eyes, and her toe tapping out a suspicious rhythm. "Did you just try to turn your horse Jaunten?"

I thought about how to answer that. Nothing that I thought of seemed likely to appease her and get me out of trouble. So I went with the blunt truth. "Yes."

She drew in a long breath. Held it. Let it out again. Her eyes rose to the heavens in a clear bid for patience. "Why?"

"I wanted to see if it would work?"

Aletha pointed a stern finger at me. "You are hereby forbidden to experiment or deliberately mix your blood with anyone else's. Do it again, and I'll turn you in to the Trasdee Evondit Orra."

"Yes, ma'am," I responded meekly. Meek was good. It would soothe her ire and make her think I was repentant.

I would need to be much sneakier with trying something in the future.

Turned out Jaunten blood was much more effective on cats than horses.

Cloud turned pure white during the course of the night. But when he woke and got back on his feet, he still had that dazed look in his eyes, as if someone could poke a stick into his ear and it would come out the other side without meeting any resistance.

I put one hand on his nose, the other on his neck to hold him still and get his attention. "Cloud?"

His big brown eye focused on me with a slow blink.

"You understand me?" I asked slowly. "Nod if you can."

He bobbed his head once.

Ha! So it had worked to a good degree. Shame it hadn't given him Tail's level of intelligence, though. Wait, maybe this was better. After all, Tail didn't have an ounce of obedience in him and had the human smarts to evade me. Did I really want to deal with a rambunctious, intelligent stallion?

Aletha might have a point. I should have thought this through a little more before experimenting.

She came up beside me, slung an arm around my shoulders, and leaned against me as she took the horse in from head to tail. "Looks like it sort of worked. I'm not sure whether to smack you or congratulate you."

I patted Cloud on the neck. "Well enough, I think. Alright, Cloud, from now on, let's work together. You know as well as I why we're here."

The horse gave a wuff of agreement, ears flickering. He looked...a little hung over, but I remembered that feeling well after waking up Jaunten. It had taken a few hours before I'd really felt like myself again.

We broke camp, saddled up, and returned to the road. Tail resumed his perch on Cloud's back and rode well there, as if he were accustomed to doing so. I eyed him over my shoulder. For some reason, he'd taken a shine to us. At several points in the night, I'd woken to find him curled up either under my blankets or under Aletha's. He acted aloof most of the time, as if he couldn't care less what we did, but he never ventured far from us, either.

Was it fear? He knew as well as I that if he were caught by a Star Order Priest down here, they would show him no mercy. He was certainly safer with us. Or maybe he just felt estranged from the other cats now, as he had changed so much. Perhaps he just felt like he belonged more with us.

I could hardly ask him to explain, all things considered. Technically, he knew how to write, though. I wondered if we could somehow rig up a way for him to hold a pen....

I looked up and found Aletha watching me with the strangest expression on her face. In the years that I'd known her, I'd seen this woman in a variety of moods and humors, but this one was new and unknown to me. I couldn't decipher it. Maybe she was still exasperated by my experimenting.

We really didn't know where to go from here. My impression of *south, body of water,* and *flat land* wasn't much to go off of. Most of southern Chahir could fit that description. Aletha suggested going to Forz, as it was a trading hub for the southern provinces and near the Elkhorn River. I had to admit, it was an excellent suggestion. It sat on the borders of Darlington, Beddingfield and Kaczorek, so it was in the right direction. Well, at least it would mean going in a southerly direction, which is what we wanted. But more importantly, it would likely have a lot of rumors flying about, so it might have some helpful information.

One could hope, anyway.

It took another two long days of being in the saddle before we finally reached the lovely town of Forz. And by 'lovely' I meant cramped, chaotic, and filthy. The city had grown from the small trading post I was familiar with two hundred years ago to this sprawling place that seemed to branch off in every possible direction. We were on something of a rise as we connected to the main highway, and from here, it looked like the outskirts butted up against the Elkhorn.

Aletha's nose wrinkled up. "*What* is that *smell*?"

"Oh, you name it, it's mixed in there." My nose gave a few involuntary twitches as a particularly strong gust of wind brought the odors of the city directly to my face. Thanks for that, wind. Much obliged. "Tanners, paper makers, city refuse, all mixed in a melting pot for our sensory pleasure."

She nearly gagged as the wind wafted over us again. "Don't they believe in sewage systems?"

"Apparently not."

The smell got worse, of course, the closer we got. Tail actually climbed up under my vest, using the leather to save his nose. Some enterprising souls had booths set up on either side of the highway selling scented masks. To anyone unfamiliar with the town, these brightly-colored scarves looked like offerings from heaven. Aletha promptly pulled over and bought two, a plain white one for each of us. I took one from her with a grateful nod and tied it around my nose and mouth.

Oh, the scent of orange blossoms. Delightful. *So* much better than the city smell. "I wonder how long these last."

"According to the merchant, it's a guaranteed eight hours or our money back." The look in Aletha's eyes said she was holding him to that promise.

We had traffic coming up and down on either side, so Aletha and I stuck close to each other, our boots overlapping. We both had our eyes peeled for trouble, because in this sort of crowd, pickpockets and the like weren't uncommon. Wagons filled with every type of merchandise, from food to uncut logs, passed by us. With them came the creaks of the wagons, the calls of the drivers, and the usual din of caravans like these.

Aletha had to raise her voice a little to be heard. "I don't see any gates or security!"

I had to rise up in my stirrups to get a good look at the road ahead. Huh, she was right. I didn't see anything either. Now, that was unusual for a Chahiran city. Or was this one of those matters where because the city sat on the border of three different provinces no one was sure who was supposed to provide guardsmen?

Knowing politics, that was likely it.

With our scented kerchiefs guarding our noses, we waded into the city proper.

"Hubby."

"Yes, wifey?"

"Might I ask a favor?"

"Anything."

"Can you not employ your usual routine of getting information?"

I put a hand to my heart, acting offended. "Me? What have I ever done wrong?"

Aletha started ticking things off on her fingers. "You started a bar fight to find a renegade priest—"

"Hey, that worked!" I protested, grinning. "And Hazard agreed it was the quickest way to figure it out."

Unfazed, she kept going, "And then there was that time when you first came onto the Red Hand, when you convinced a double agent that you were actually a *triple* agent—"

"I had that well in hand until I got ratted out."

"—or perhaps I should remind you of that lovely incident when you hired yourself onto an assassin's payroll in order to sneak inside a building?"

"Ah, good times, good times." Frowning, I added regretfully, "I doubt there are any assassins here."

Aletha lifted her eyes to the heavens and muttered, "Thank the Guardian of the World for small favors. My point is, please, when you go asking for information, try not to start any bar fights or turn any other cats Jaunten?"

"You're simply taking all the fun out of this, dearest."

"I live to put a spike in your wheel."

Not bothered by this warning, I smirked. "I'll do my best."

"That's what I'm afraid of." Without glancing back, she said in a nonchalant tone, "Tail? Feel free to scratch him when he starts misbehaving."

Tail purred in a rumble of agreement.

"Hey!" I glanced between them, brows furrowed. "Seriously, since when did you two get to be on such good terms?"

"Secret," she purred, sounding strangely feline.

I gave her a suspicious look out of the corner of my eye.

The highway we were on dumped us onto the main street which had vending stalls and open markets clustered together on both sides. There was absolutely no sense to how everything was laid out. Food stalls were right next to blacksmith shops, cloth-

ing shops next to junk stalls, farmers' tables butted
up against physicians' clinics. I couldn't begin to sort
it out. How did anyone shop here without feeling lost
the entire time?

"Farmers first," Aletha suggested.

I raised my eyebrows at her. "Why them?"

"Farmers pay attention to the weather more than
anyone else. With the possible exception of sailors."
She shrugged. "Surely they would be the ones to notice a change."

"Excellent point. Since it's your idea, will you do
the honors?" I waved her forward.

She guided her horse over to the nearest farmer's
table and leaned down, carefully asking them in her
best Chahirese if the weather had been strange in the
past few weeks. The two old men looked at each other
and then shook their heads, silently saying they hadn't
noticed anything. But the young girl actually manning
the table—I took her for a granddaughter—piped up
with, "But you said it's been raining more than it usually does, Granda."

"It's not been *that* much more, Celli," he objected.

She got this mulish set to her jaw, eyes narrowing.
"You *said*."

He held up a wrinkled, gnarled hand. "I know, I
did. We get a few more inches of rain, a farmer notic-
es. Been good for crops. But it's not what this lady is
asking. She wants to know if there's stormy weather
ahead, and we ain't seen that."

Aletha gave them a sweet smile. "Even rain is bad
news for a traveler. Thank you, both of you. Can I

have some of those apples?"

We could've used the extra travel food, no doubt of that, but that wasn't the main reason why Aletha bought a little something. It was always good form to repay information in one way or another. So my mission-wife bought six apples, paid more than what they were probably worth, and then we moved on to the next stall.

I personally find it very unfair, but a pretty woman can always get more and better information than a man can. Even one as charming as me. So as we went from stall to stall, I hung back and let her do the asking. This place was such a mix of people that I even saw a few Hainians and other Solians in the crowd. Aletha wouldn't meet with any southern prejudice here. This might be the last time she could openly ask such questions though. When we hit the smaller towns and villages, they would be much more suspicious of a foreigner.

I trailed along and kept an eye out for pickpockets, letting her talk and charm and shop. Women were naturally gifted at multi-tasking, so she did all three at once with ease. In between the traffic, tradesmen calling out wares and prices and such, I couldn't always hear her or the replies that she got. But I noticed that in between stalls, she started to frown in growing puzzlement. Oh? Not getting the answers that she wanted, or not getting answers that agreed with each other?

We finally got through that street and fetched up at the main fountain in the town center. I hadn't expected to see such a large, decorative fountain in such a shabby, thrown-together town like this one. But someone had invested in it and put in some very pretty blue tiles, making an arcing wave pattern around the base. We pulled up to it and dismounted, giving our backs a rest from the saddles and the horses a well-deserved water break.

"Well?" I asked her. "I couldn't always hear you or the answers you got."

"For the most part, it was very conflicting." Aletha put her hands on her waist and stretched backwards, arching to relieve the ache there. "I think I can see the overall pattern, though. Where's the map?"

I went to Cloud's side and dug through a saddlebag. It didn't take much digging, as the map usually stayed on top one way or another. It had seen a lot of travel and was worn around the edges, but it was still perfectly readable. I passed it over without a word.

Aletha sat on the edge of the fountain and smoothed the map out over her knees, preventing it from getting splashed. "I didn't think to ask this of the first two farmers' stalls, but the other seven were from somewhat different areas. Two of them were from near here, and they hadn't seen any difference. But the others were from farther south, more toward the Kaczorek/Beddingfield areas, and they *did* notice the weather had changed in the past two weeks."

"Changed badly?"

"Just changed. Most of them were happy about it, actually. It meant more rain, so their crops are better this year than usual."

I rocked back on my heels and thought about this.

"Is this a significant enough change to warrant it being magical? Or not?"

"Now, that *is* the question, isn't it?" She frowned down at the map. "But right now, it's the only clue we have."

"So where were these farmers from? Exactly?" I leaned forward to get a better look.

"Hubby."

"What?"

"You're blocking my light."

"My bad." I took a step to the right, bumping into Cloud a little when I did so. "So, where again?"

She traced a line near the Beddingfield/Kaczorek border. "Along here. Now, they weren't from very far away."

"No surprise, they can't travel far without their produce spoiling, after all."

"Right. But the farmer who experienced the most difference in the weather was the one farthest out."

I hummed and thought about it. "So we really do need to get farther south? Busted buckets, I was hoping that my large body of water was the Elkhorn River."

"You and me both." She stretched out her legs with a grimace. "All this riding gets old after a while."

"So...you're thinking that the body of water we need is the ocean?"

"Or it's still the Elkhorn, just farther down. The Elkhorn *does* dump into the ocean, right? So it goes all the way to the southern coast. Who knows? She could be anywhere along the river."

"Right. Well, should we head towards Bedding-field, then? The only major highway in the area skirts along the Beddingfield/Kaczorek border anyway."

"On one condition."

"Name it."

"Let's get a decent meal first?"

I laughed but had to agree. A person could only eat so much travel food before they just had to have a real meal. "Sure, why not?"

For the next three days, we just rode south. I kept my eyes on the landscape we traveled through, comparing it with the image that the Gardener had given me, but it didn't match up. It slowly started to, though, as we passed through the greener farmlands and into the drier, rockier landscape of southern Chahir.

Midafternoon of the fourth day, the coastline of Beddingfield came into sight. At this point, the land almost looked right but it didn't *feel* right. As much as I wished that the Gardener had known the human name of the place and simply given that to direct me, I had to admit there were perks to his method of direction. It wasn't just the way the land looked, but the way it smelled, the air about it. I had no doubt that when we finally came to the right place, I'd know it instantly.

Of course, that assumed I went in the right direction to find it.

We stopped in sight of a fishing village that rested on top of the shore. It didn't seem to be a particularly prosperous place, as it barely had twenty houses all huddled together and only four fishing boats docked. I was of two minds about going anywhere near it as people from rural, small villages like this were not tolerant of strangers. They certainly wouldn't look kindly on foreign strangers like Aletha.

But in truth, we were short on food and had to get it from somewhere.

"Gorgeous, I don't think it wise for you to go in there."

She studied the place through narrowed eyes. "I think you're right. I'll sit tight here while you buy some food. See if you can't get some information too."

"Will do." With a tap of the heels, I urged Cloud toward the village.

Distance had definitely made the place look better than it was. 'Shabby' didn't even come close to describing it. Everything was clean though, without any refuse or garbage in sight. I got many a curious look as I rode through the one and only street in town. But then, I'd have gotten strange looks in a crowded city. A white-haired man, on top of a white stallion, with a white cat riding comfortably on the horse was bound to attract attention.

There was a large well in the center ring of houses, and since I didn't see any signs of a tavern or inn, that was where I chose to stop. I dismounted with a creak of leather and a sigh, as it felt good to be on my own feet for a while. A middle-aged man with dark skin and thinning blond hair cautiously approached me.

"Yar name, sar?"

Whew, talk about an accent! It was thick enough to slice up and serve on bread. "Shad," I responded with a smile. "I wonder if I could buy some traveling food from someone here. I think I have a ways to go yet and I'm runnin' short on vittles."

At the word 'buy' he brightened up perceptibly. "Sure, sure. I'm Vick. Leave the horse thar and come with me."

I dropped Cloud's reins on the ground and murmured for his ear alone, "Stay. Do not go off with anyone. Tail, guard him." It was sad, but I trusted the cat more than the horse to remember simple commands.

"Whar ya headin'?" Vick inquired, leading me to a nearby home that seemed marginally more prosperous than the others. Well, at least this one had glass windows instead of thin wax paper.

"Now, that is the question," I admitted, making up a story on the spot. "You see, my family was from this area and I stayed here often as a boy. But then my parents moved farther north and died some years afterwards. I thought to come back down here, look up the rest of my family, but I don't remember the name of the village. I've been searching all along the coast for a place that looks familiar."

We ducked into the house and I had to blink several times to adjust to the dimness. A lean, tough-looking woman looked up from the bread she was kneading and gave me a suspicious look. "Vick?" she asked in a husky voice.

"Traveler wantin' to buy some vittles," Vick responded as if she had asked a full question.

She perked up at the word 'buy' as well. "Sure, sure. I've fresh bread, a wheel of cheese, and fish jerky that should travel well."

Fish jerky? Who'd heard of fish jerky? My mouth wasn't sure what to think about eating something like that. But it beat having nothing to eat at all, so I nodded amiably. "Sounds fine."

"How much ya need?" she asked me.

"However much you can spare," I responded carefully. "I'm not sure how far I'm going."

She gave me an odd look. "What sorta man travels without knowin' his destination?"

"He's looking for his childhood home and kin," Vick supplied. "He don't rightly remember the name of the place, just what it looks like."

"Ahhh." She nodded sagely, as if she'd heard of something like this before. "Sar, yar family name?"

"Warr," I said, picking out the most common name in all of Chahir.

"Many a village has Warrs in it," Vick commented, stroking his chin thoughtfully with his palm. "Not helpful, that. What's the place look like?"

I described what the Gardener had given me, being as exact as I could.

Vick nodded a time or two, but never interrupted. At the end, he gave a gusty sigh. "Now, I know a few places that look like that. Seen 'em while I'm fishin'. Mostly towards Aboulmana, near the coastline."

My attention sharpened on him. "I need to head

further west, then?"

"Nothin' like what ya say if ya go east, towards Kaczorek," Vick assured me. "Not for a hundred miles, leastways."

Was I ever so glad I'd come in and talked to this man. He had just saved me a lot of traveling if he was right. And since he'd been fishing and sailing around these parts his entire life, he probably was.

His wife tied up the food in a clean cloth and handed it to me. I was generous when paying them, as it wasn't just the food but the information they gave. With a smile and word of thanks, I stepped back out and headed to Cloud. So, we needed to go west. Good. I liked having a firm direction rather than just flipping a coin to decide.

When I went back outside, I found Tail sitting on the saddle, glaring at everyone around. There was something of a crowd, roughly a half-dozen men staring in bemusement at the cat. When I lifted the reins, one man was bold enough to ask, "Sar, ya mean that's yar cat?"

I smiled at him with easy confidence. "It sure is. Well, that is to say, he decided he likes me and he's been following me around ever since."

"Ah," he nodded in understanding. "When a cat adopts ya, a wise man just goes along with the flow."

"Nothing else to be done," I agreed. The crowd started to disperse as I remounted Cloud. Tail hopped back to his usual spot as we rode out of the village and rejoined Aletha.

She had been lying on the ground, comfortably

propped up as she enjoyed being out of the saddle for a while. At my approach, she quickly rolled up to her feet. "Well? How'd it go?"

"They weren't as hostile as I'd feared they'd be," I answered. "I got bread, cheese, and fish jerky."

Aletha blinked at me, head cocked. "Fish jerky? Never heard of it."

"Makes two of us. Hope it tastes alright." I'd feed it to Tail if it didn't.

"I second that. Any information?"

"I spoke to a fisherman and he said the area we're looking for could be in Aboulmana. He said there's several places along the coast that look like that."

Her eyebrows arched, interested. "Oh? So we need to go west, then? Good, I like having a direction. You said that the impression you had of the place included a lot of water nearby. Maybe it was the sea instead of the river."

"Could well be." We wouldn't know for certain until we found the place. "At any rate, let's head west."

I held up a hand to shield my eyes from flying dust and debris, grimacing as my ears started to ache from the constant wind. "Wifey!" I shouted over the howling.

She was only a little ahead of me, so she didn't need to do more than look over her shoulder and shout back, "What, darling?"

"We've got to get out of this storm!" I had experienced this once before. It hadn't been down here, but much farther north. The wind had been inescapable, unrelenting, and the flat area we'd been in had no cover to offer. Being battered by the wind like that wore a man out, left his ears aching for days, and often got something sharp and unpleasant lodged in his eye.

Here, in this gently rolling grassland, we didn't have a lot of options for shelter either. But we'd been passing little ravines here and there, and if we hunkered down in one of those and staked the tent overhead, we'd be out of the worst of it. Right now, that sounded like a splendid option.

Aletha must have read my mind, as she pointed ahead to a ravine that wound near the road. It had a gentle slope to it on one side, easy enough for the horses to use, but wide enough in parts that we could all fit onto it. I gave her a nod, signaling that I liked it too, and we made a beeline for it.

Even with us shouting, we could barely hear each other, the wind snatching at our words. I gave up talking to her about three sentences in and fell to hand signals, which she understood perfectly well. We'd been working with each other for so long that we didn't need to communicate a lot anyway. I could more or less anticipate what she would do next, and she the same of me.

In short order we had the tent unpacked, the horses temporarily settled in the ravine. Just being down here cut the wind chill in half. I no longer felt like a man being battered on all sides.

Unraveling and staking out a tent in a windstorm was quite the trick, let me tell you. It was akin to a beaver building a dam during a typhoon. It almost took off on us several times, and only by leaping on top of it did I prevent it from flapping away into the sky. By sheer determination, we managed to stretch it over both sides of the ravine, one of the dirt walls hemming it in and letting it have enough support that it didn't budge. I still staked it so hard into the ground that the tops of the stakes were depressed *into* the dirt a little.

In relief, we climbed inside. Well, I did take the precaution of wrapping cloth around the horses' eyes first, just to prevent them from being hurt. I didn't think they would though, it was *so* much better down here. When I got into the tent, tying the flap firmly behind me, I noticed that Aletha already had my bedroll and hers rolled out, our food pack open and half its contents strewn about in a semicircle.

"Shad, almost everything we have requires a fire to cook it," she informed me with an unhappy pout.

"You want to start a tent fire by cooking in this wind, be my guest," I invited her cordially. "But do warn me, as I'd rather be a good ten feet away when you do."

Shaking her head, she started putting food back in. "No, thanks, I'd rather be a little hungry than deal with that wind."

Couldn't argue there.

Since we didn't really have anything to do and it

was fairly late in the evening anyway, we just ate a cold dinner before settling into our bedrolls. We were both soldiers, after all, and we understood that we should take advantage and sleep when we could. Tail seemed to agree, as he found a corner of my bedroll and curled into it, falling almost instantly asleep.

No matter how firmly we'd strapped the tent down, the center of it still flapped above our heads, although not enough to risk smacking someone. It was as noisy as a flock of upset magpies. The horses, not liking the noise or the wind storm raging around us, shifted uneasily and whickered to each other. Between their restlessness, the noise of the flapping tent, and my worry that our shelter really would take off, I found it hard to go to sleep.

"Shad."

Apparently I wasn't the only one. "Hmm?"

She rolled onto her side and put a hand on my arm, body coming in close enough that I could feel the heat of her skin, although we didn't quite touch. "I don't want you to go."

Go? Where? Oh, she meant— "Why, darling, I'm touched."

Blowing out a breath, she admitted sourly, "I realize that it's selfish of me, but a part of me wants to ask that you stay in Ascalon."

I grasped her hand and sighed, not sure how to handle this. My teasing had not had the desired effect. "We both know that if Garth actually *asked* for my help, he's at his wits end."

"He's gotten better at communicating since he got

married, though."

"Well, sure. Wives have that sort of effect on their husbands. Or so I've seen." From this angle, I could only see the top of her head, but the way she tightened her grip on me, and the odd inflection of her voice, told me how upset she really was by this. For the first time, I really *felt* my decision to leave, and I had to admit, it left me feeling...strange inside.

"Aletha, I have to go. I can't *not* go. This first generation of magicians cannot be lost. Chahir can't afford that. We must safeguard them, and the only way to really do that is to teach them how to defend themselves."

"Who are you trying to convince? Me or you?"

"Yes," I admitted wryly.

She let out a year's worth of sighs. "I suppose you don't have a choice anyway, not with the task the Gardener set for you. You're right, once you have that girl, you've got to protect her for the foreseeable future, at least."

"Right? So I have to be at Strae, one way or another."

"Have you decided what you'll be to her?"

Sometimes Aletha and I were so in sync that we could finish each other's sentences and know what the other was going to do before they even started moving. But other times, like now, she'd ask me a question and I hadn't the foggiest notion of what she was thinking.

"Come again?"

"What you'll be to her," Aletha repeated, eyes

studying my face. "No, I can see you haven't given it a thought. Seriously. Men."

"Darling, before you go on your usual rant about a man's denseness, do you mind explaining? With lots of small words, if you will."

Even as she rolled her eyes, she was smiling at my dry tone. "Shad, my love, you do remember how hard it is to leave behind everything you've ever known, going off with complete strangers, into a world that makes no sense to you?"

"Ahhh..."

"She's only around eight years old and that's a lot for an adult, much less a child, to handle. Wouldn't it be better for both you *and* her to have a firm grasp on what your relationship will be to each other? If she knows what you are to her, she'll trust you more, but it'll also give her a foundation. Say, an older brother, or an adopted father, or a crazy uncle." She paused before adding thoughtfully, "You'd excel in the role of crazy uncle, actually."

I preened at the praise. "Why, thank you, darling."

"My pleasure," she returned with a coy bat of the eyelashes.

I thought about her suggestion and realized that she was right. I'd been so focused on trying to find the girl that I hadn't really considered what to do with her once I had her. But the feeling of being lost in a new world, surrounded by people I didn't know...oh, I remembered that vividly. "Which should I offer to be, do you think?"

"I'd let her decide, actually. It'll sit better with her

if she has the choice."

Women hated having decisions made for them. Even miniature ones. I would be wise to take that advice. "Right. I'll ask her, then."

"If at any point, you feel lost about how to raise her, I'd ask Garth for advice."

Yup, she'd lost me again. "Uhhh...why Garth? He's not a father."

"No, but he has an amazing example. His father is one of the best I've ever seen."

One of the reasons why Aletha had joined the military at such a young age was to escape her home life. Her father had been an astonishingly cold and domineering man up until the day he died. I'd met him once, and I didn't have a favorable impression of him. Aletha hadn't shed a single tear at his funeral, and after hearing what her childhood was like, I didn't blame her. So saying this about Arden was high praise indeed. "I'll do that."

Silence fell for a time before Aletha spoke again, voice strained and thin, "You're so set on moving to Strae, but...you won't regret leaving?"

I sensed by the tone in her voice that this was not the moment to joke and so gave her a straight answer. "Of course there will be some regrets. I'll miss you terribly."

Aletha lifted up onto an elbow to look at me. "You mean you'll miss me cooking for you."

"And covering for me when a prank goes wrong," I continued with a growing smile. "And having a ready sparring partner, not to mention someone willing to sneak into places no sane person would attempt. It's hard to find someone who matches your own brand of crazy, after all. Life is going to be so much more boring without you."

"Thank you." A beat. "I think. But even knowing that, you'll readily jump into this?"

Should I tell her this or not.... Well, Aletha and I didn't really keep secrets from each other, and it might let her accept my decision more if she understood what I was thinking. "I was actually going to take Garth up on his offer before I even made contact with the Gardener," I confessed.

"What?" she demanded sharply.

"Aletha." I rolled onto my side to meet her eyes. "I love working with you, and the rest of the Hand, but Ascalon is not home. I've tried to make it so, but it just hasn't ever felt right to me. Chahir is in my blood, I guess. It doesn't feel right living on foreign soil."

She slapped a hand against the ground, looking frustrated, but at the same time, she didn't really look surprised. More resigned. "Xiaolang said we wouldn't get to keep you for long. Curse him and that empathic ability of his. He's never wrong about things like this."

So Xiaolang had seen this coming, eh? That didn't surprise me. The man knew a lot about the people around him but was amazingly good at keeping secrets. I was surprised he'd said as much as he had to her. Well, him already suspecting where my heart was would make it easier to hand in that formal resignation later.

Speaking of Xiaolang...that enigmatic smile of his

when we'd first set out still played in my head. I wasn't able to make sense of it even now. I had no doubt he sensed something that I needed to know. In fact, that smile put me strongly in mind of the one he'd had back when I'd confronted Garth about his touchy-feely policy with Chatta.

I blinked at my own thought and played that memory through my head again. Yes, remarkably similar.

Huh. I looked down at the woman lying next to me with new eyes. Aletha had fallen silent, but the downward curve to her mouth said that despite the answers I had given, she was still upset about this whole thing. Could she...possibly be...?

I wet dry lips and tried to subtly test my theory. "Have you ever thought about leaving Ascalon?"

Whatever she'd expected me to say, that hadn't been it. She gave me a very blank expression. "Leave Ascalon?"

"I know you've lived there most of your life, and you even enlisted when you were sixteen, but...well, you seem to enjoy it whenever we travel into a different country. Have you ever thought of trying to live somewhere else?"

"I have, actually." There was an odd note in her voice when she responded, and she gave off the impression that she was carefully choosing her words before speaking. "Recently, I've thought about it a great deal."

"Is there anything holding you back from trying it?"

"It's more like, I don't have the right motivation to try it. I would need some compelling reason to leave behind the life I've built. Besides, if Xiaolang lost *both* of us at once, I'd better have a very good reason ready before resigning."

"Good point." That was an interesting response. She sounded open to the idea, but not, at the same time. I didn't know what to make of it. I didn't know what to think of any of this, actually, or how to respond to what she'd said, so I fell silent.

Once again, it was Aletha that broke the silence, although this time she had a teasing smirk on her face. "Shad, there's something I think you've failed to consider about all of this."

I'd been thinking about it for a fairly long time, actually. I couldn't imagine how I'd forgotten any angle of it. "What's that?"

"When you become a professor, you'll have to be a role model to your students."

I blinked at her stupidly. "Role model? Me?"

"That means you'll have to obey all the rules and set a *good* example," she clarified. In this dim lighting, it was hard to tell, but I'd swear a devilish twinkle was in her eye.

I put a hand to my forehead, groaning. "Perish the thought!"

"I'd sooner bet that the moon will turn red than you can manage to behave for more than five minutes," she continued thoughtfully. "I wonder how long it will take before Garth regrets offering you a job."

"Ten minutes, surely."

"If that."

A moment of silence fell before Aletha once again broke it. "Now that I think about it, you as a role model scares the light right out of me. What was Garth thinking?"

I just laughed.

How had this happened *again?*

With a curse and a cough (the latter being a futile attempt to get fur out of my mouth), I abruptly sat up, dislodging my furry bed partner. Tail gave a disgruntled hiss at being so rudely jarred awake. I glared right back at him. "How did you get inside my blankets?"

Issuing me a haughty stare, he turned his chin up at me and ignored the question. With an arch of the back, he stretched his way out of the blankets before sauntering off, no doubt in search of breakfast.

I followed his retreat with my eyes. Obviously, drastic measures were called for in order to keep him out of my bed. I would have to be careful about it to avoid inviting revenge.

Thinking evil thoughts, I went about getting my own breakfast cooked, feeding Cloud, and generally breaking camp. Aletha never laughed aloud, but I knew she was laughing on some level, as she kept having to turn her face away from me, like she was fighting a smile. I aimed a glare at her back. Somehow, in

the course of the past nine days, she had succeeded
in making some sort of deal with Tail that kept him
out of her bedroll. How, I didn't know, as it certainly didn't involve food. He was regularly bringing me
things to cook for him.

I kept an eye on her as we worked, still wondering
what last night's conversation really meant. Aletha
had been on the verge of telling me something, I felt
that to my bones, but what? I could hazard a guess or
two, but wasn't sure. What she had said last night, and
Xiaolang's sideways hint, had me thinking though.

It made me question for the first time: What did I
really want?

Ever since escaping that crystal, I had more or
less been jumping from one situation to the next, trying to find my footing in this strangely familiar world.
Perhaps I had developed a bad habit over the past
two years of simply reacting. Being the guardian to a
Weather Mage would certainly limit my choices for
the next decade at least, granted, but I still had room
for wants and desires of my own, surely.

Maybe it was time I really started to think about
things instead of simply going where the wind blew
me.

By the time I was saddled up again and ready
to go, Tail had reappeared from his venture into the
grasslands, licking his mouth clean in obvious satisfaction. Aletha and I mounted up and headed onto the
road again.

As the morning progressed, it became increasing-
ly obvious that we were not on a major highway and

were well outside of any city's boundaries. The road winded about on a whim; it was full of potholes and the grade was far from even. Since it was still better than trying to forge through the briars and brambles in the grasslands, we stayed on it.

We left the grasslands completely somewhere around noon and abruptly hit forests. In fact, we had so many trees and such around us that I was beginning to doubt Vick-the-fisherman's directions. The image in my head didn't have any trees in it whatsoever. Were we really supposed to go this way?

By midafternoon the mystery solved itself. We left the last of the trees behind and exited out onto a semi-rolling country that seemed to be an endless stretch of grass and outcroppings of dark brown boulders. I took in a deep breath, surprised to finally see the land I had been searching for. When I did, the distinct smell of water and the slight tang of salt filled my nose. The smell of the place, the look of it, the *feel* of it, clicked into place with me like a missing piece fitting into a puzzle.

"Aletha."

She reined to an abrupt stop, her head whipping around, eyes wide with surprise. But then, I only ever used her name when it was important or somehow serious.

"What?" she asked sharply.

"This is it." My mouth curled in sharp satisfaction. "We're here."

When the Gardener had said that she was 'lost,' he hadn't been kidding. Just where by all the saints and gods was she?!

I scrubbed the back of my head, beyond frustrated. This was the right area, I was sure of it. It matched the picture that the Gardener had given me. But we'd walked all through this fishing village without even a hint of a girl that looked like our Weather Mage. For that matter, it didn't look like they even had any girls the right age to be her. So what was going on?

Aletha sidled up next to me and whispered in my ear, "Maybe this isn't the right place?"

I shook my head. "It's right." Well, no, not quite. I took a slow turn in the middle of the street, looking all around me. Something didn't feel right. The people here weren't welcoming of us, and we were getting a lot of wary looks from the locals, but that was to be expected. What I couldn't explain was how they shied away from all contact with us. We were on the coast, they couldn't be *that* cut off from the rest of the world to where any stranger was an oddity.

This vibe felt familiar. Wrongly familiar. It reminded me of when we were in Jarrell, and Choi, where the people were so harsh and closed off. I silently motioned Aletha to remount, and she gave me a grim nod of agreement before swinging back onto her bay stud. I climbed back onto Cloud as well, Tail lightning leaping out of my way and onto his usual perch as I swung the stallion around and quickly left the village.

As soon as we were out of earshot, Aletha let out a loud, pent-up breath. "Phew! I didn't like the feel of that place at all. You know what it reminded me of? That village in Farless that was executing whole families left and right on the suspicion of having magical ancestors."

"Me too," I agreed grimly. I twisted about in the saddle and gave the village another long look. It was a semi-prosperous place actually, and some would have called it a proper town. It even had a few brick buildings instead of every house made of wood and seastone. This place had the first paved streets I'd seen, although it was crude stonework and cement, nothing fancy. Still, they were doing well enough from outward appearance. So why did it feel so disturbing?

"Shad, something that Asla mentioned to me a week ago has come to mind." Aletha inclined her head toward the village. "She said that a lot of the southern villages, the ones far from the capital cities, still harbored Star Order Priests and teachings."

I blinked at her. "I thought that was all settled."

"Oh, the main priests and ringleaders are all accounted for. But the initiates? The followers? The devotees? There's no way that you can find all of them. Right now, the Star Order won't look kindly on anyone they don't know, especially since Vonlorisen has been borrowing a lot of manpower from Hain in order to hunt them down."

True, if looked at from another perspective, Aletha and I could easily be mistaken for a pair of investigators or Hainian informants. I said a few choice words under my breath. "That explains it. But if that's the case, then our girl mage can't be anywhere near the town."

"She'd have been discovered long ago and killed if she *had* stayed," Aletha agreed. "So, she's well out of the sight of the town. Now, you said she looked like she was about eight or nine?"

"Right."

"So where would a child hide from the scary priests?"

Now that was the question of the year. "She has to be somewhere in this area," I said slowly. "The Gardener would not have pointed me here unless he knew she'd *be* here for me to find. I know he said she was lost, but I think he meant she was lost from the eyes of men."

"But lost how?" Aletha threw out a hand in an expressive manner. "I mean, look at this place! It's all low hills and grass until you reach the coastline! You can't hide anything out here."

"And the coastline is riddled with nooks and crannies, probably quite a few caves." I shared a speaking look with her. "A girl who grew up in this area would probably know a few of those caves."

"It's the most logical place to start looking." She rubbed at her chin thoughtfully. "But if you were a priest, wouldn't you look there too?"

"Well, sure, as it's the logical conclusion. But I have the strangest feeling that she hasn't been caught yet. Maybe she knows the area well enough to hide away from them. Or maybe they've assumed she's drowned, or run farther away."

"That's a lot of maybes," she pointed out.

"Don't I know it. But my gut says to check the coastline."

She raised her shoulders in a shrug. "We might as well. We have to start somewhere, and it doesn't look like anyone in that village will talk to us."

Unfortunately true. We could've really used a little information right now. Just a hint would have sufficed. I blew out an irritated breath and guided Cloud's head around. "Let's go spelunking, shall we?"

We found a switchback, narrow trail that meandered from the top of the rocky shoreline to the equally rocky beach below. With care, we descended, the sea breeze whipping our hair against our faces as we went. It felt good in a way, as it cooled off the intense heat of the summer sun, but it also felt like the salt was stripping a layer of skin off. By the time we reached the beach itself, my clothes were slightly damp from the spray and stuck to me unpleasantly.

Tail let out a mewl of disgust and snorted, ears flat

against his head.

"Believe me, we don't like it either," Aletha informed him, her nose wrinkled. "What is that *smell*?"

"Dying-sea-creature, I do believe," I informed her mock-cheerfully. "Flavored with decaying kelp and rotting-something-or-other, all for your sensual pleasure."

"I'll skip the delight, thanks."

Surely our noses would get used to it and we wouldn't notice it anymore. Until then, I couldn't help but wrinkle my nose as well.

"I wish our scented handkerchiefs were still working."

"You and me both," I muttered.

Scent.

I blinked as the thought hit me. "Tail. You can smell better than humans can, right?"

He gave me a long look that said, *Duh*.

"As strong as a dog?"

Tail flipped a paw up as if saying, *More or less*.

"Then, can you smell if there's any people down here?"

"Oh, that's a good thought!" Aletha chimed in. "Tail, maybe you can find her. Do you sense any human children down here?"

Tail's nose lifted and he sniffed into the wind for a long moment. Then he lightly leaped down onto the dark shoals and started off, heading directly west.

I cackled like a mad hen. I had a Jaunten cat and I knew how to use him....

If anyone had been watching they'd have thought

we were barmy for sure. Two humans leading their horses while following after a white cat as it leaped confidently from one boulder to another, crossing over little tide pools and going around small waterfalls. We had to slow down several times, calling for Tail to wait, as we figured out how to get the horses through the area. Sometimes the beach disappeared completely, leaving only narrow footing in shallow water, so by the time we'd gone any distance at all, Aletha and I were soaked from the thighs down. Tail, unfairly, still managed to find a way to lead us without dipping a single toe into the water.

He was quite smug about it, too.

After following him blindly for about an hour, I was starting to think that he was just messing with our minds—cats were prone to do that—until he jumped on top of a boulder and went abruptly still. His ears swiveled back and forth, but his eyes remained fixed on a spot dead ahead.

I caught up to him, motioned for Cloud to stay put, then clambered up on top of the rock, next to where he sat. "Well? Did you find...her...." My words dried up.

There, not ten feet away, stood a little girl. She had a fishing net at her feet, as if she had been trying to do some catching in the shallow pool nearby, but now she stood directly facing us. Her curly blond hair was a tangled mess around her face, skin slightly red from the sun and dirty with grey streaks, her blue smock and leggings not in much better condition.

But in spite of all that, I recognized her instantly

from the image the Gardener had given me.

Finally. *Finally*, I'd found her.

I was so relieved to see her, whole and unharmed, that I leapt off the boulder without thinking and started toward her. She instantly backed off a pace, eyes narrowed.

"Wait," Aletha warned me in a low whisper.

I let out a breath and reined myself in. Patience. I had to be patient. Who knew what she'd gone through in the past few days?

"Hey there, sweetheart." I eased down to one knee in an effort to keep from looming over her. She eyed me with considerable wariness, a fishing knife in one hand. I didn't doubt the sharpness of that knife or her willingness to use it. Of course, a young girl wasn't going to pose much threat to me, but the goal here was to earn her trust, not her wrath. Still, I liked this show of spunk. When danger knocked on her door, she met it head-on. This was my kind of kid.

With a thumb, I pointed at my own chest. "I'm Shad. I've come on behalf of the magical school, Strae Academy, to come get you."

At 'magical school,' she lost about half of her wariness. In fact, I could've sworn from the look on her face that she was expecting me. Her grip on the knife didn't loosen though. "And her?"

"Ah, I'm a friend of his," Aletha introduced herself pleasantly. "My name is Aletha. When Shad said he was coming down here to rescue you, I came along because I was worried about him going alone."

Of course, as a non-magical person, I wouldn't

have a clue about any of this, but I tried saying something I'd heard Garth say before. "She won't glow to you. But me, the cat, and the white horse will look faintly red."

Oh, that rang a bell with her, alright. Her eyes went wide in her face.

"...How'd you know?"

"We're all Jaunten, you see," I explained with my most charming smile. "A mage, like you, can see the magic on us."

She didn't drop her guard altogether, although I was definitely making headway. But then, the Star Order Priests would have been able to do and know the same things I did, so she wouldn't think it odd for me to know these things. To her, I could still be a danger. I tried to think of a way to convince her to trust me. Odd, as much time as I'd spent on the road actively searching for her, I hadn't thought I'd be trying to win the girl over.

Alright, when in doubt, start at the beginning. "I've been looking for you for a solid week, pretty lady. A Gardener came to me, you see, and told me that a mage had awakened in Chahir. I was to come get you, guard you, and take you to Strae Academy so that you could be trained safely."

Those stunning blue eyes of hers narrowed suspiciously. "What's a Gardener?"

"They're a very special race of people." I rubbed at the back of my head, wondering how to explain something as complex as a Gardener to a child. "They're about your height, but they have skin like white marble, and their hair looks more like fine feathers. They are the caretakers of this world. They keep the land flourishing, and healthy, and sometimes they step in and take care of people too."

Ohhh? She looked excited about this, as if she recognized some part of what I was describing.

"Do they talk in your head?" she asked intensely.

I blinked. How in the world had she known that? "Well, they have to touch you to do that, but yes, they do. They like to speak in images, too."

"I met one!" Her wariness dropped instantly, as if it wasn't ever there. "Are you the Guardian?"

"You *met* one?" Aletha repeated incredulously. "When?"

"A week ago," she answered confidently. "I was going to run away, like Mama said to do, but then he came and talked to me. I thought he was my age at first, 'cause he was so little, but he was *lots* older," she said this as if imparting a secret. "He showed me my cave and said to wait there, as a Guardian was coming."

Well, well, so I wasn't the only one he'd visited. "That'd be me," I said with a slight bow. "Might I know your name, Princess?"

"Shabeccaan." She took two careful steps forward, eyes scanning my face. "Becca, for short. You...are you really my Guardian?"

"I am." This poor child. She looked as if she were on the verge of shaking, she was so afraid. How much courage did it take to face two armed adults with only a fishing knife in hand? "I'll protect you from any harm that comes near you. You have my word as a Riic on that."

That was all she needed. Tears welled up in her eyes and her knife dropped from numb fingers. I knew what would happen next with absolute certainty and quickly crossed to her. Becca let out a wail, part relief, part despair, and started crying in earnest.

I scooped her up and held her tight. Her tiny arms went around my neck and clung on for dear life as she started crying into my shoulder. My heart went out to her, and I didn't try to halt her tears, just let her cry it all out. If I had been abandoned by my parents, with Star Order Priests after my life, I'd be crying too.

Aletha looked up at the sky. "We don't have a lot of daylight left. Let's take cover in her cave tonight and set out tomorrow."

Not a bad plan. Becca was crying too hard to give us directions to where the cave was, though, so I went with the next best thing. "Tail. Lead us to her cave. Don't give me that look. I realize you're not a hunting dog, but you're the best thing we have."

He sniffed the air in several directions before sauntering off confidently over the rocky shore, heading for the cliffs. Since I had my arms full, I looked back over my shoulder and ordered Cloud, "Follow."

We all trailed after the cat like we were playing some sort of follow-the-leader game. Tail didn't once pause or look uncertain, so in spite of his protests, his nose did as well as any tracking dog.

Becca finally relaxed her death grip on me and eased back enough to wipe at her cheeks with the back of her hand. I dipped a hand into my pocket and brought out a handkerchief, which she promptly used to blow her nose with. After all that crying, her eyes were red and puffy, but at least she didn't look on the verge of falling apart anymore.

Turning, she looked at Tail with a puzzled slant of her head. "He understands you?"

Hmm. "How much do you know about Jaunten, Becca?"

"They're scary people," she responded promptly. "They have magic and they work for the King of Hain. That's it."

As rumors go, at least this one had mostly gotten the facts straight. "Well, we *can* be scary to our enemies. Lucky for you, we're on your side." That won a faint smile. "We don't have magic so much as we're touched by magic. See, we inherit all of the knowledge of the people whose blood we share. So I know everything that the past sixteen generations of Jaunten knew."

That impressed her. "Really?"

"Really. Now, because I accidentally mixed my blood up with Tail's—that's the cat—he's now as smart as a human."

"*Really?*" Her eyes went as big as saucers. "Magic can do that?"

"We're just as surprised," Aletha assured her wryly. "We didn't know it would work on animals either until a few days ago."

Becca twisted in my arms to look over my shoulder. "So, the horse is smart too?"

"It didn't work quite as well on him," I confided in a whisper. "But he certainly got smart*er*."

"Oh." She pondered on that for a moment. "I guess it works better on cats."

"Seems so," I agreed. I wondered at this conversation, as in her shoes, I'd be asking very different questions. But maybe she couldn't handle anything too serious right now and so chose to talk about different things instead. I decided not to push her. She'd been under too much pressure already.

"What's your full name?" she asked me.

"Riicshaden," I responded promptly.

Becca started, jaw dropping. "Like that famous soldier who was locked up in a crystal?"

I was just as startled. That story had made it all the way down here? "You've heard of me?"

"That's you?! How'd you get out of the crystal?"

"A friend of mine got me out," I answered, deciding on the simple version of the story. "He's an Earth Mage, so it was easy for him."

"Oh. Have you been out a long time?"

"Almost two years, now." It didn't take a telepath to see what she was thinking. I grinned at her. "You're really impressed now, aren't you, 'cause you have a legend to guard you."

She nodded dumbly, still speechless.

I just chuckled, my ego stroked that she really had thought that.

"Hey, illustrious soldier, if you don't pay better attention, you're going to slip on these rocks and head feet-first into the ocean," Aletha drawled.

I shot her a dirty look. "You just had to take me down a rung, didn't you?"

"At the rate you were going, your head would've swelled too much to fit into the cave," she pointed out evenly. Her eyes were laughing at me, though.

Aish. With friends like her, who needed enemies?

"Captain Shad?" Becca ventured in a cautious tone.

"Just Shad is fine, sweetheart," I assured her. "What is it?"

"Um, you said I'm a mage? Do you know what kind?"

I paused in my tracks and met her eyes. "Yes. You're a Weather Mage."

"A Weather Mage," she repeated in a breathless whisper. "Am I powerful?"

"Amazingly so. Becca, listen to me, as this is very important for you to understand. You are the *last* Weather Mage. You are the only one in the world." She looked like I'd smacked her in the back of the head. "Do you understand me? If you are lost, the world will never have another Weather Mage again. Do *not*, whatever you do, put yourself in danger. Always call for me if there's trouble. We cannot lose you."

"I'm the only one?" she repeated, face wrinkled into a bemused frown. "But I thought there were lots of mages."

"Not all mages are the same," Aletha explained. "Each mage is capable of only one thing, one type of magic. They can't do everything like witches or wizards can. You know that magic is inherited?"

She cocked her head. "It is? So my family can be mages too?"

"No, just you," I corrected her. "You're the only one in your family with that talent. But it's very possible for your children and grandchildren to be Weather Mages."

"Oh." She chewed on her bottom lip as she thought about that.

Hmm. We might have given her a little too much information at once. It had to be a lot for a child to take in. Most adults needed time to adjust after hearing all of that.

I focused instead on getting us under cover.

The sea was cooler than I'd expected it to be in high summer, and the mist that hit us as we walked close to the shoreline felt like small icicles stabbing into my skin. I shifted Becca from my left side to my right to avoid getting her drenched from all the spray. Aletha had been correct that the rocks were slippery, and I had to watch where I put my feet. Tail, naturally, navigated it without trouble. The two horses trailing after us did slip a little with their hooves scrambling to find purchase. But they managed to get through the roughest spots and back onto the gravelly beach without breaking a leg.

Becca made that squirming motion that all children did when they wanted down, so I obliged and set her back on her feet. She gave me a shy smile, pink in her cheeks, before she darted forward. "This way," she encouraged over her shoulder.

Aletha murmured from the side of her mouth, "I detect a case of hero-worship developing."

"Kid has good instincts," I praised with a cocky smirk.

With a long sigh, she just shook her head. "Poor girl. She doesn't realize yet what she's getting into."

Becca had carved something of a niche into her cave, and it felt strangely welcoming inside. She had a small fire going near the entrance, its flames burning low to avoid letting much smoke out. A shallow depression in the cave floor had been filled with water so that she had her own miniature pool to store fish in. It looked rather empty at the moment, with only one fish swimming lazily about, but she had three cooking on the embers. Before doing anything else, she promptly turned them over with a practiced turn of the wrist, preventing them from scorching.

A little further inside was a nest of blankets and a traveling cloak, all laid out neatly. She had a dress hanging from a rocky protrusion, and it looked damp, suggesting she'd just washed it. I approved of these cleanly habits. At least she'd been raised well.

"Come in," she encouraged us. "There's a place at the back where it goes wide," her arms stretched out in illustration, "and the horses can fit there."

"Sounds good," I agreed. "Cloud, go with Aletha."

Aletha led them to the very back, their hooves making sharp clattering noises against the smooth rock underfoot. I snatched my bedroll and saddlebags from Cloud's back as he passed me and looked around for a place to settle for the night. I didn't want to get too far from that cave entrance, as someone needed to keep a look out.

To my surprise, Becca went directly to Tail and sank down onto her haunches to put them at eye level. "Hello. I'm Becca," she greeted.

Tail flicked an ear and bobbed his head to return the greeting.

"Are you hungry?" she asked him in genuine concern. "Do you want some fish?"

The cat visibly brightened. Becca didn't need a translator to understand that expression and instantly scooped a piece of fish from the fire and presented it to him.

I bit the inside of my cheek to keep from laughing. An instant friendship had just been forged. No matter how much human intelligence he might have had, it didn't replace his instincts. To cats, whoever fed them was a friend. Of course, by doing that, she'd just volunteered to be that cat's personal chef for the rest of her life. After all, he had to blackmail me into cooking for him. She was an easier mark.

He daintily devoured the fish in quick bites, picking it completely clean. I kept an eye on them as I settled in. Becca seemed content for the moment to just sit there and watch him eat, occasionally reaching over to stroke his head.

I could hear the purrs from over here.

She had to be starved for human interaction. A week was a long time to go without having anyone to speak to. No wonder she naturally gravitated to the cat.

When Tail finished, he climbed into her lap, rubbing his head against her chest, still purring. Becca openly beamed at him and started scratching under his chin, which *really* got the purrs going.

Aletha returned with her bedroll and saddlebags slung over a shoulder, took in the sight of the happy Tail, and cocked her head in question.

'She fed him,' I mouthed carefully.

Her mouth formed an 'ahhhh' of understanding, eyes crinkled up in amusement.

I paused in midstep on seeing that expression. It was the first genuine smile I'd seen from her for some days now, ever since our late-night conversation.

Aletha watched the heartwarming scene for a few moments longer before turning and making her own spot. I kept an eye on her as I did the same. I still didn't know exactly what I wanted, or how to go about getting it. And while I was glad to have found Becca, having her here did complicate the situation somewhat.

We still had some food supplies of our own, so we brought them out and started making dinner. Becca hovered near my elbow, her eyes glued to the vegetables and bread that I sliced up. But then, after a solid week of nothing but fish to eat, she would probably give her eye teeth for some variety.

We ate in companionable silence, with her consuming anything we handed over. This lack of curiosity on her part felt strange to me. Did she not want to know where we would go and what we do after this? Or did she feel that she couldn't ask for some reason?

Aletha must have thought the same things, as she ventured, "Becca, we'll leave here in the morning and take you to Strae Academy."

She froze with her mouth full of food. Carefully swallowing, she glanced at both of us, eyes wide with unease. "Where's that?"

"The very northern part of Chahir, the Isle of Strae," I answered. What did that expression mean? "It's a new magical academy that King Vonlorisen had built. The Earth Mage I mentioned earlier, the one that got me out of the crystal? He's the one that built it, actually, and he runs it now. He'll take good care of you and make sure you're trained."

"So you'll guard me until then?" Her voice shook as she asked.

It was the nuance behind 'until then' that cued me in. She'd been told a guardian was coming to protect her, and I'd said I would do whatever it took to keep her safe, but at no point had I told her how long that would last. Did she think I was temporary? That I was only here long enough to take her to a safe place?

I could see it in her eyes, how scared she was. But what child wouldn't be scared to leave everything they knew, everyone they cared for, and go to a place she'd never even heard of? Aletha's advice had been dead-on. I needed to give her something, some foundation that she could hold on to; otherwise I wasn't sure if her heart could take this.

So I knelt to put us on eye level and gave her a grin. "Hey Becca, didn't you know? I'm supposed to protect you for the rest of your life."

She swallowed hard, eyes staring at me hopefully. "You...you'll stay with me? Forever?"

"Yup, sure will. Now, it's your decision what you want me to be." I counted out the options on my fingers. "One, father. Two, crazy uncle. Three, crazier brother. Which one do you like?"

Whatever she'd expected me to say, it wasn't that. She had the blankest expression on her face that I'd ever seen. "But...we're not related."

"Adoption, kiddo, adoption. Haven't you heard of it? I'm saying, adopt me as your relative. You get to choose what kind I'll be."

She mulled that over before glancing at Aletha, as if wondering just how serious I was about all of this.

Aletha nodded in support. "I know it's hard sometimes to tell when he's joking, but right now he's serious. He really was sent down here to rescue you, but he was also ordered to protect you and make sure that nothing *ever* happens to you. So you can take him at his word, Becca."

Her eyes fell to the ground as she thought all of it through. I waited patiently, not in the least interested in trying to hurry her along. This was one decision that I wanted her to make without any outside influence.

Finally, she lifted her head and looked at me with

complete soberness. "You're too young to be my dad-dy."

Well, she had me there. At the ripe old age of twenty-five, I was a bit young to have an eight-year-old daughter.

"You're too young to be my uncle too," she added firmly. "So, older brother."

"Older brother it shall be, then." Not that we looked the least bit alike, but whatever.

"Speaking of family," Aletha interjected. "Becca, I think we should tell your parents that we have you and where you're going. Right now, it's dangerous to have any contact with them, but later on, you might be able to. What do you say?"

Becca perked up at this idea. "That'd be good."

"I don't think you should leave the cave," Aletha continued thoughtfully. "Too risky."

"I can't go back," Becca said firmly, although her eyes were sad. "I can never go back there."

I studied her from the corner of my eye. Now, that was an interesting reaction. Most children would be looking for an excuse to go home, but she steadfastly refused.

Aletha caught it as well, eyes narrowed slightly in an expression of perplexity. "Yes, I know. But you tell me any message you want to pass along and I'll deliver it."

I looked at her askance. Of the two of us, I'd pass better in that village than she would. So why was she volunteering to go? "Wifey, you sure?"

Aletha gave me a reassuring nod. "It'll be near

sunset by the time I climb back up there. I've gotten into more fortified places with less cover than this."

Well, granted, she had a point there. But I could tell from the expression on her face and the significant look that she gave Becca what her real reason was. She didn't think it wise for me to leave Becca right now, and I had to agree with her. The kid didn't openly cling to me, but the way she never got more than a foot from my side spoke volumes.

Becca thought for a moment before she gave Aletha a message for each member of her family and directions to the house. Aletha listened attentively and repeated it all back to make sure she had it. When they were both satisfied, she picked up her sword and silently exited the cave.

Watching her go, Becca asked uncertainly, "Will she be alright alone?"

"Sweetie, I feel sorry for anyone that picks a fight with her," I chuckled. "Now, let's get these dishes washed and you in bed. We've got an early start to make in the morning."

Aletha ducked into the cave with nary a whisper of sound. I only knew she came in because I was keeping a very careful watch on the entrance. She caught me watching her and whispered, "Hey."

"Hey," I returned just as softly, aware of the sleeping child at my side. "So?"

"I ran her parents down," Aletha responded without preamble. She sank next to me, curling up comfortably on her bedroll with her legs tucked up next to her. "You want the long or short version?"

"I think I need the long one."

"Right, long it is." Aletha's expression became cold and smooth, like a stone carving. I immediately tensed. I'd seen that expression before. I'd never liked what happened afterwards. "So, two weeks ago, when she started showing signs of her mage ability, the Star Order Priests were immediately contacted."

I still found it hard to swallow that parts of Chahir still clung to the old ways so ferociously. I knew that they were here, and active, but it seemed more *real* now that I was down here.

"Fortunately, the mother had enough love for her daughter to make up a quick plan. She put together food and supplies for Becca and ordered her to make a run for it. Disappear, don't contact anyone, and head straight for the capital."

My eyes nearly crossed. "She ordered an *eight-year-old* to run away all the way to the capital?" There were full-grown adults I didn't trust to cross that kind of distance alone!

Aletha nodded grimly. "It gets better. After she sent her daughter off, she made up a story about how they went fishing together and an accident happened, so that the girl died and fell into the sea. The whole village believes her dead."

Hence why Becca was so adamant that she

couldn't enter the village. Got it. If she went there, it would destroy the cover story her parents had concocted. But still, what kind of mother sent her daughter off into danger alone? "What, someone couldn't go with her?"

"I think they're scared of her too," Aletha admitted, and she looked as if she had bitten into something rotten while saying the words. "The prejudices run strong and deep here, Shad. We're lucky they had enough parental love for her to even give her a fighting chance."

I looked down at the girl curled up around Tail, peacefully asleep, and couldn't agree with Aletha. What kind of fighting chance does an eight-year-old have of traveling the road across the country? "This is so many levels of wrong I can't even begin to count them all."

She let out a long sigh. "That's rather how I feel about it. Strange, we spent over a year in this country hunting down budding magicians and rescuing them, but I still haven't gotten used to how cold and cruel people can be here."

I was born in this country and I couldn't fathom it either. But I didn't want to.

Silence fell between us for a time. Aletha stirred, leaning forward so that she could see over my legs and look at the young mage. "So, straight back to Strae?"

"That'd be best," I agreed. "Well, we actually need to head straight out of Chahir. We're closer to the Hainian border than anything else right now, and I think the faster we're off Chahiran soil, the better."

"Couldn't agree more," Aletha sighed. "Ye gods, I'll be glad to leave this place behind. How do you want to go?"

"I think we should try to catch a boat going up the Elkhorn River. It'll get us to the safe house outside of Waterford that way and it'll be easier and faster than trying to hoof it over land."

"Sounds fine to me. Do you want first watch or second?"

"I'll take first."

"I'll turn in, then."

Yeaoooooow!

In sheer instinct, I flailed awake and staggered to my feet in a little under a second, only to curl forward, pain throbbing in my groin. I glared murderously at the cat that had, only a moment before, landed on me with claws extended. Tail glared right back at me, back arched with his fur standing straight up. "*Must* you have clawed me *there*?" I demanded around a sleep-clogged throat.

"*Shad,*" Aletha hissed from the cave entrance.

I snapped around, eyes searching for her in the dim lighting of the cave. I'd barely been able to see Tail before, only focusing on his glowing eyes. Aletha was little more than a silhouette against a starry backdrop. "What?" I demanded in a low whisper.

"I count three Star Order Priests coming towards us, fast. There might be three more behind them, I can't be sure of the number. The rocks are blocking my sight."

"Already?" I responded in resignation. I'd have

thought that we would have at least eight hours or so of safety before we needed to leave. But, I suppose that had been wishful thinking. A white-haired man, riding a white horse, with a white cat, must have sent all sorts of alarming signals to the locals. As paranoid as they were, they'd have called the priests just because of my general strangeness.

"I'll get the horses," she said, racing for the back of the cave.

I shoved my feet into my boots. "I'll get Becca."

I didn't bother trying to wake the sleeping mage, just grabbed her and hauled her into my arms. Of course, she woke up from being rudely jerked out of her bedroll.

"Wha—" she managed, hands grabbing my shirt in sheer reflex, finding her balance.

"We've got to move, sweetie." I mentally scratched off most of our equipment as lost and steeled myself to somehow replace it later. Right now, my priority had to be getting out of this cave.

Caves are simply wonderful for giving shelter to weary and stranded travelers. But in a strategic sense, they're equally terrible. They are the worst fatal funnels in the history of fatal funnels, as not only do they force you to fight in a narrow area, but they end at some point, leaving you no escape route. If I didn't manage to keep the entrance clear, Aletha would be trapped back there.

I made it out of the cave, trying to stay low and in the shadows, but of course, Becca lit up like a beacon for the Star Order Priests. They didn't need their normal vision to see her. One of them gave a shout, calling to the others that he saw her.

Growling, I set her back on her own feet, my eyes never leaving the enemy running toward us. "Becca, listen to me. When Aletha gets out here, you climb on board the horse with her and you *run*. Don't look back, don't try to help, just get out of here."

Her hands clung to mine in a startlingly strong grip. "What about you?" she asked, voice shaking. "There's lots of them."

I had perhaps twenty seconds before they were on top of me. I took ten of those seconds to reassure her and gave a cocky wink. "You remember who I am? What the legend said about me?"

"Gran said you were the best soldier ever. No one could beat you."

Did the story really say that? Should I correct her? I actually had been beaten a few times…naw, probably shouldn't mention it. "That's right. You don't need to worry. I've fought priests a lot stronger than these before. You just go."

Aletha chose that moment to appear, the reins of her horse in hand. She grabbed Becca around the waist without pause and threw her into the saddle before climbing quickly on board as well. "Shad?"

"Be right behind you," I promised.

The moon was just bright enough out here that I could see her mouth curve into a frown. Then she looked at the girl sitting in front of her, at the priests, then back at me. It was reluctant, but she nodded in understanding.

I in no way underestimated Aletha's skills. She was experienced with fighting Star Order Priests as well. The only reason why I stayed to fight them off, preventing them from staying on our trail, was this: I was faster. I had a better chance of defeating all six and not letting any one of them escape.

Aletha set her heels against her mount's flanks and set off as quickly as she could over this rocky, slick ground. I unsheathed my sword and settled into a fighting stance.

"Hey, you gormless pillocks!" I greeted cheerfully.

"You scrubber!" the nearest priest yelled back. His face was in shadow, so I couldn't see much of him except for a tall, lanky frame, but his voice sounded fairly young. "You have no right to insult us!"

"You lot of wazzocks just came to kill my little sister, and you think I won't hurtle a few insults at you?" I threw my head back and laughed.

"She doesn't have an older brother!"

My grin became feral. "She does now. I am Riicshaden of Jarrell. Fight with me, you manky skivers."

All my taunting worked on most of them. Of the six approaching, four came directly at me, their staffs held at the ready. But two were either wise enough or just experienced enough to realize I was only taunting them to keep everyone away from pursuing Becca. They didn't rush, but tried to get closer to the waterline, bypassing me and heading for the narrow trail that led back toward the top of the cliffs.

Of course, I couldn't let them do that.

In a burst of speed, I sprinted to the side and

cut them off sharply, my sword coming up even as I planted my feet, snapping the staff aimed at me up and away. I was close enough to see his eyes, how they widened in surprise at the suddenness and fury of the attack, but I gave him no time to collect himself. I slammed my knee up toward his chest, and more importantly, toward the staff angled in front of it. The metal guard that I had over my shin and knee gave me enough strength to snap the staff in half.

With a soundless sigh, his eyes rolled up in the back of his head and he slowly slumped to the ground. I recognized the reaction instantly—the priests at the Hapt-den-War Pool had reacted the same way when I'd broken their weapons, as they had magically linked to them in order to gain a fighting edge. Pity that didn't work on me.

But if they were *all* linked to their weapons like this, then the fight just got a whole lot easier.

I couldn't spin on my toes like I wanted, or do the quick bursts and side-steps that I was used to doing, because this uneven ground made it hard to keep my balance. But even still, I managed to twist and catch the next priest that was rushing toward me with a quick jab. He dodged it, narrowly avoiding a foot of steel in his gut, but I hadn't planned for that attack to do anything anyway. Instead, I went for his feet, dropping low and kicking his knees out from underneath him. He tried to use the staff in his hands to keep himself upright, but that just meant I had the perfect leverage and angle I needed to kick it and break it neatly in half.

It snapped with a very satisfying *crack*.

Two down. A smile lit up my face as the blood started pumping and that old, familiar surge of adrenaline really started coursing through my veins. Nothing was quite like this moment, when everything seemed crystal clear and somehow in slow motion at the same time.

In that moment, I heard something that I shouldn't have. The low, rumbling growl of a massive storm coming in fast. I dared a peek over my shoulder toward the sky. Strange, I'd never seen a storm move in that fast and furious before. In fact, it was very unnatural how the whole thing seemed to come out of nowhere.

At that moment, I remembered something, a trivial detail that I hadn't focused on before: Becca's magic was active.

In other words, I had a child mage on my hands.

Shrieking hinges!

Cursing myself aloud for forgetting, I went for the next priest with more energy and fury than was probably necessary. Even as I fought, spun, parried, and retaliated, I was mentally castigating myself for being three types of fool. If I had just thought to ask, I wouldn't have come down here without at least one magician and a few sealing amulets. As it was, I was going to have to travel through dangerous country with a nervous and upset child Weather Mage.

I chopped the next staff cleanly in half and sent another priest sprawling.

The storm arrived overhead and instantly let out

sheets of rain. In seconds all of us were drenched right down to the skin. Rivulets of water streamed from my bangs and into my eyes, which pretty much blurred my vision. If that wasn't bad enough, strong winds came with the storm, whipping everything around us and throwing rain into our faces. I went from being able to sort of see in the dim lighting to not being able to see my hand in front of my face.

Never mind fighting, I wouldn't be able to walk straight in this mess!

Blowing out a breath, I mentally shrugged in resignation. Well, this should prove to be an interesting fight.

In this storm-swept beach, I didn't have a prayer of finding my opponents, much less fighting them. I could only hope that they were just as lost and confused in this as I was. I felt my way along, one hand up to shield my eyes (a more or less useless gesture on my part) as I moved back toward the cave. Cloud should be around here somewhere, unless he'd gotten confused and followed along behind Aletha. I really hoped he hadn't, but that horse couldn't be described as the sharpest tool in the drawer.

As I slowly put one foot in front of the other, one hand outstretched in front of me, I had to wonder how the girls were faring in this mess. They had Tail with them, so supposedly he could guide them through safely. If they could see him. I was certainly banking on Cloud's superior ears and nose to get me to them, as I couldn't see a single thing here. I felt like a blinded bat.

My hand slammed into something slick and un-yielding. Cliff face? No, wait, it felt warm. I put both hands against the surface, brushing sideways, and felt the distinct sensation of wet fur. Whoo-hoo! Found Cloud.

"Cloud!" I yelled over the fury of the storm. "Track the girls! Understand? Take us to the girls!"

I felt his neck tense and relax as he bobbed his head, signaling he understood. He stood patiently and still as I used my hands to find the saddle, and the stirrup. With a practiced heave, I relied on muscle memory to swing aboard him. Of course, I failed to consider what might be on the other side.

Without warning, I slammed my foot toe-first into the rocks. Hissing in pain, I cursed aloud and quick-ly withdrew my foot, which left me in an awkward half-mounted position. Cloud shifted ever so slightly underneath me, as if wondering what I was doing. Still growling and grumbling, I gingerly put my left leg down again, feeling my way this time so that it went in between the wall and the horse's side. Only then did I feel around and slide my boot into the other stirrup.

Untying the reins from the pommel, I slapped my heels into his sides and urged him silently to go. The reins I just let rest in one hand, as they were more or less useless in this situation anyway. I couldn't guide him when I couldn't see anything.

I could've really done with a hat right about now. That would've at least kept the rain out of my face. It had to have been a good twenty minutes or so since the storm rolled in, but it hadn't abated in the slightest. This definitely couldn't have been a normal storm.

Chatta had explained to me once that magic followed intent more than anything else. That was why young magicians had to go through so much schooling and training, to discipline their own minds so that they could guide their magic in proper ways instead of just running off their own instincts. Right now, I appreciated the need for teaching magicians more than ever before. Becca had to be running scared. Her instinct was to hide, to somehow defeat the scary Star Order Priests and prevent them from ever finding her. A mother storm like this one would surely do the trick, which was why she had instinctively called for it.

But it also came with complications. The storm might keep the priests from finding her, but it might also prevent *me* from finding her, which was more than a little problematic. It also obscured all those handy landmarks that I needed to navigate by. Aletha and I had planned on reaching the mouth of the Elkhorn River—which was relatively close by—catching a boat, and riding it up and into Hain. In this crazy weather, we were likely to ride right past it without even realizing. Travel problems aside, by using her magic she was even brighter and more obvious than before to anyone with magical ability. It would be especially easy right now to be found by any priest looking for her, at least with their magical senses. Of course, he'd have the same trouble as me tracking her down in this muck.

Try explaining all of that to her instincts, though. It wouldn't work. That was the trouble with instincts—

they often fed into one feeling at the expense of something else.

I slicked the hair back from my face in a gesture of frustration. What to do? Assuming I caught up with them, I would have to find some way of either reassuring Becca so that she naturally stopped summoning this storm or find a way to turn her magic off for a while.

Unfortunately, I only knew of one way to do that.

I'd probably traveled in more miserable situations than this, but at the moment nothing else sprang to mind that could top it. Cloud and I both were soaked to the bone, rivulets of water streaming into our eyes and near blinding us, wind strong enough to set the ears to ringing. The wind coming up from the sea, had a distinct chill to it, which made goosebumps rise along my skin. I would've given my eye teeth for a cave right now. I'd give more than two teeth for a fire to go with it.

On top of this mother storm making things un-bearable while traveling, it completely skewed my sense of time. I would've sworn that we'd been trudg-ing along this winding path for a decade, but it was probably closer to a few hours. The sky had lightened somewhat, indicating that the sun had risen. I hadn't spent much time beating the priests, so I would have thought that we'd have caught up with Aletha and Becca by now. We hadn't. And that worried me.

Cloud *had* understood me, right? Or had he lost

their trail in this wet, muddy madness? He hadn't faltered or paused, so I'd thought he'd known where to go. But then, I'd named him Cloud for a reason. Perhaps I should rethink this blind trust I had in his tracking skills....

Sheer instinct had me ducking, hugging Cloud's back, as an arrow whistled past where my head had been.

I could think of two types of people that would be out in this crazy weather. Hoping it was the one I wanted, I sucked in a lungful of air and bellowed, "GORGEOUS! DON'T SHOOT!"

"Shad!" a faint, familiar voice responded from up ahead. Aletha stepped around a tree and came into view, sort of. The day had lightened up enough that the path ahead looked dim, but I could see silhouettes, at least. She waved a hand at me in greeting, a bow and arrow held ready in her other hand. How she'd managed to use that while getting pelted by rain, I didn't know. After all, water and bows did not mix well. Wait...she had that water-repellant bow Chatta'd made her, didn't she? I'd nearly forgotten she had that.

Cloud, still on orders, took me directly to Aletha without worrying about stray arrows flying about his head. He stopped in front of her with a pleased swish of the tail and glanced back at me, eyes saying, *Didn't I do good?*

"You did great," I praised him, patting him on the neck. "Good horse."

"I'm amazed he managed to track us in all of this,"

Aletha observed, also reaching out to pet him on the
nose.

"Wifey," I said mildly, dismounting, "shouldn't
you have called out and made sure it wasn't me before
shooting?"

She shrugged, unconcerned that she'd nearly put
an arrow in my forehead. "Well, I figured it this way.
If it was a priest, it would be one less to worry about.
If it was you, you'd duck."

"I find your faith in my dodging abilities a tad
alarming, darling."

"Why? You ducked, didn't you?"

"There's a hole in your logic somewhere. I just
can't put my finger on it." She unabashedly smirked
at me. Shaking my head, I let it drop and focused on
more important things. "Becca?"

The little girl came out from behind Aletha, her
arms shielding Tail from the worst of the rain. He still
looked like a drowned rat, though. Becca's eyes lit up
in relief when she saw me, and she bounded forward,
stopping just shy of touching me. "Shad!"

"Hi there," I responded, smiling slightly. "The
scary priests are all defeated and won't come chasing
after us. So set your mind at ease, eh?"

She nodded, then bit her lip uncertainly. "Aletha
says my magic is doing that." She pointed upward
towards the sky. "But I can't turn it off."

"This happens with young magicians," I assured
her patiently. "My Earth Mage friend said he once
nearly uprooted a forest because of a bad dream. It's
not something you need to be scared of or worried

about."

"But..." she trailed off and looked upwards again.

"True, it's not making traveling any fun," Aletha pitched in supportively. "But it's also obscuring our tracks and making it hard for anyone to find us. So it's helpful in that way."

"Oh." Becca thought that over before she finally relaxed a little.

I'd prefer to have her magic settle again into that docile mode where it didn't stir up the weather, because at the moment, it wasn't doing anything more than messing up our travel plans. I slicked a hand over my hair and looked around.

"Shad, do you have any idea where we are?" Aletha asked, also looking around, brow furrowed in confusion.

"Chahir," I drawled.

I got quite the stink eye for that.

"Along the southern coast," I added helpfully.

Becca poked me in the thigh reprovingly. "Be serious."

"Now, I ask you, where is the fun in that?"

For some reason, both women gave me an unamused look.

Sensing that my humor had missed its timing, I gave a put-upon sigh and tried to behave. "No, I don't know precisely where we are. I have a bad feeling that we missed the highway leading to the Elkhorn River, though."

"In the dark—" her tone added, *and in this raging storm*, "—it would be easy to miss. I estimate that we've been riding about eight, nine hours straight."

No wonder my stomach was clamoring for attention. Not that we could do anything about that now. We had no equipment to cook with, even if we could stop and take the time to hunt something down. "In that case, we're several hours past the highway. Curses."

"Shad, Garth said the old safe houses were back in commission, right? Isn't the nearest one dead east of here?"

"Aletha, that's another two days' ride!" I protested. "Most of it through mountainous terrain, as we have to cross the Black Ridge Mountains to get there!"

"We lost all of our supplies," she pointed out with ruthless logic. "We're not going to be able to pick up much from these local fishing villages. We should avoid them as much as possible anyway, as they're just as likely to call the priests on us as the last group was. We're not supplied enough to make a trip across the country. Our best bet is getting to the safe house and letting them help us. Or going into Hain proper and having a magician there ferry us to Strae."

I shook my head before she could even finish that sentence. "And risk Becca falling into the hands of the Trasdee Evondit Orra? No way. Garth has more or less wrested all of the Chahiran magicians away from them, but I don't think even he could get Becca back if they ever got their hands on her. He told us point-blank on the way down here that even having her in Strae would be a major battle."

Becca inched in closer to me, huddling against my

legs. "Are they bad people?"

"Not bad," I assured her with a wry twist of the lips. "Just...greedy. Some of them are good people, but some of them aren't, and I'd rather not take chances with you. If they ever got their hands on you, you'd never be allowed to leave Hain. Being wet and hungry for another day or so won't kill us. I'll take my chances with the safe houses, but we're not going any deeper into Hain than that."

Aletha was aware of the politics as much as I, and she gave a reluctant shrug of agreement. "Probably wise. Let's mount up, then. The sooner we get to shelter, the better."

I couldn't disagree.

I'd harbored a secret hope that when Becca saw me alive and well that her instinctive call on her magic would calm and the storm would break up and go away.

Alas, it was not to be.

Aletha's reassurance earlier had not been a lie. The storm *did* cover our tracks, washing them all away and making it impossible for a normal tracker to find us. However, that didn't hold true for the priests. They, after all, had a way of tracking magicians miles and miles away. Especially with Becca openly using her magic like this, she would blaze for them. The storm was like a giant, glowing sign pointing toward our location.

I waited a good five hours, traveling along with her, waiting for the storm to abate. It didn't. In fact, it might have gotten a little worse. Our uncertainty of where to go, the lack of supplies, and the way we wandered these back, twisting roads did not set Becca's mind at ease.

Unfortunately, half the problems we had were a direct result of her magic being used. I had no other choice. I had to turn her off.

Lifting her up by the waist, I turned her sideways in the saddle. She looked up at me, head cocked, not understanding what I wanted. My mouth twisted up in a sorry smile. "Sorry, kiddo. No choice. I'll make it up to you later."

Her brows furrowed, not at all understanding what I meant by this.

Not about to explain, I simply lifted my hand and chopped her sharply in the back of the head. Her eyes rolled up before she abruptly slumped forward, out cold.

"Shad." Aletha's tone had a disconcerting mildness to it. "Did you just knock her out?"

"No choice," I sighed. "It's the only way to turn her magic off."

"What?" Aletha spurred her horse forward to ride next to me. The trail didn't really have the width for that, so her knee jammed right next to mine at an uncomfortable angle, but she didn't back off and stayed right there. "What are you talking about?"

"Unless a magician anchors a spell, if they lose consciousness, their magic stops." I had a weather eye on the sky as I explained, waiting to see how quickly the storm would dispel. "That's why Garth had to stay up those few times when he had a shield up over us in Chahir, camouflaging our camp. He couldn't anchor the spell—it would leave too much of a signature behind—but he couldn't sleep either, or the spell would break."

Aletha regarded the little girl slumped against my chest. "True, it's all-around better for her magic to be dormant again, but...did you have to do it that way? You couldn't wait for tonight, while she sleeps?"

"And risk the priests following us straight to our camp tonight? Again? You *do* remember they have ways of tracking magic that can go over miles, right?"

She held up a hand. "You're right. I just don't like the idea of manhandling her like that."

"I don't either," I admitted morosely. Even though I had very good reasons for doing it, I still felt guilty, and a phantom ache had settled into my hand. "I kept hoping that with me back, she'd feel reassured enough that her storm would go away on its own. I didn't really have a choice. We can't keep traveling like this."

Shrugging agreement, she looked up at the sky. Already the rain had stopped, the wind had dropped down to a light breeze, and the clouds were starting to break up. The storm was disappearing as fast as it had appeared.

With the clouds no longer obscuring the sun, we could see our surroundings much better. We had—

somehow—managed to enter the Black Ridge Mountains without realizing it. At least, the way the trail sloped abruptly and the amount of trees surrounding us suggested as much. Where we were exactly, I hadn't the foggiest. Hopefully we'd stumble across a landmark, or a town, soon and be able to get our bearings.

Pointing at Becca, Aletha inquired dryly, "And how exactly are you going to make it up to her later?"

"Shhh. I'm thinking."

"Uh-huh. Good luck with that."

Without a storm obscuring our vision or a magical beacon drawing in pesky Star Order Priests, we made much better time. The roads were clogged with mud and small streams, of course, so the path could hardly be described as *clear*, but it still beat riding through a mother storm.

Becca slept peacefully in my arms as we wound through the mountain trails. Tail sat on the back of Aletha's horse and openly glared at me.

"What?" I demanded finally. "I didn't have a choice, alright? Her magic was out of control and I'm not a magician, I couldn't help her turn it off."

Tail let out a disgusted mewl.

"Oh, so you have a better suggestion? No? Then what are you blaming *me* for?"

"I'm not sure which worries me more," Aletha said to the air in general. "The fact that you're arguing with a cat, or that you understand what he's saying."

"Please, as if it takes any talent to know how mad he is at me for hitting his girl."

Tail's eyes narrowed to mere slits and his ears went flat on his head, fur rising on the back of his neck. I recognized the warning signs clearly. At some point, in the dead of night, he *would* get his revenge.

We came around a switchback bend in the trail that led directly to a rather substantial road that bordered on being a highway. I stopped at the edge and looked both ways, but it remained open, broad and relatively mud-free. Someone had gone through the trouble of putting pea gravel down and some sort of hardened mud that made the road firm.

"I didn't expect to see something like this here," Aletha observed, tone openly delighted. "Are we near a major town or something?"

"We must be getting close to Rykern." Jaunten knowledge said as much, anyway. "It's a famous logging town. Most of the lumber that you see on the southern edge of Chahir comes from it. It's been a major settlement for decades now."

"Oh, so the wide road is for them to ship lumber out of the mountains?"

I nodded confirmation even as I used the sun to get my bearings. "We're probably a little north of the town right now. I say we go down, get supplies there. Who knows? We might even be able to hitch a ride on one of their ships and get around to a major port that way."

"Several weeks at sea beats land travel," Aletha agreed fervently. After all, on a ship, the priests couldn't get at us. We'd be much safer on the ocean.

Of course, the trick would be avoiding suspicion

long enough to get on the boat. If they even had a boat. There were too many ifs in all ofs this for my peace of mind. "So, cover story. We're a young family traveling to visit my relatives and we got lost in that mother storm last night?"

"Our equipment got lost in the process of us trying to find shelter," Aletha added.

"And we're tired of riding like this, so we're look-ing for a boat to get us to the next main port, which will cut down on our travel time."

"Most of it's not even—technically—a lie."

"The best cover stories have a little truth in them." I grinned at her and got a grin in response.

Aletha pointed at Becca with her chin. "And have you thought of what to tell her when she wakes up?"

"I'm waiting for a brilliant flash of inspiration."

"Ahhh." Aletha nodded with mock-wisdom. "How's that going for you?"

"Not well," I admitted cheerfully.

"I suggest you think of something quickly. We'll have to wake her up before we hit the town."

My smile stayed in place, but my heart sank. The odds of me thinking of something appeasing in the next few minutes were not good.

I think…I was in trouble.

There are two creatures in this world that you

do not want to ever upset. The first are women. The second are cats.

I knew that the universe must've been especially pulling my leg because at this precise moment, I had *both* mad at me. The bribes I had bought to pacify them weren't working either.

Sitting back on my haunches, I looked at the two of them for a long moment. We'd managed to find a good inn that had a rather spacious room. Aletha went and bought clothes, equipment, and such while I babysat Becca and Tail. We more or less spent our time washing up while waiting for her to get back. Then Aletha had taken a turn at the baths while I ducked out and bought bribes. Unfortunately, the delectable salmon I bought for Tail and the new hair clasp for Becca did not succeed as planned.

So here I sat on the floor, while they were huddled on one of the beds in our room, steadfastly not looking at me.

Becca's mouth formed a pout even as she clutched Tail tighter to her chest. "You *said* the storm helped."

Actually, Aletha had said that…no, don't correct a woman in a bad mood. That was one of the cardinal sins of the universe. "It did help obscure our tracks," I agreed. Busted buckets, I'd hoped that an apology and a shiny present would smooth this out, but apparently I would have to *talk* my way out of this one. "Becca, sweetums, here's the problem. The priests, you see, have a way of detecting magic when it's being used."

She froze and peeked at me from the sides of her eyes. "They do?"

"Yup. And they can detect it from *very* far away. The stronger the magic being used, the easier it is for them to track it."

Biting her bottom lip, she asked uncertainly, "How far is very far?"

"We're not entirely sure of the range, but over twenty miles."

Her eyes went as wide as saucers. "Twenty *miles*?"

"Sometimes farther, depending on what tools they're using," I explained, glad she was listening and not still pouting. "If they have a big scrying pool, they can see the whole country. If they're using something else, then the range is a lot smaller."

She repeated 'country' silently, looking more than a little terrified. "So...so when I called the storm..."

"You were shone like a beacon on top of a hill. Anyone could have seen you." I spread my hands helplessly. "I'm not a magician, sweetheart. I don't have any sealing amulets or spells that would subdue your magic and make it hard to find you. I just didn't have *time* to prepare for this journey like I should have. And because of that, the only way I knew of making your magic turn off was to make you fall unconscious. If it comes down to a choice between your safety or having you mad at me, I'd rather you be safe and mad at me." Giving the cat in her arms a narrow look, I added, "All of which *you* know, so why are you mad at me?"

Becca and Tail shared a speaking look, and I swear to you, they were having a telepathic conversation on whether to forgive me or not.

Thank all gods, saints, angels, and pink elephants, they finally did. I knew they did because Tail squirmed free of Becca's arms and went promptly to his fish, where he started daintily devouring it. Becca picked up the hair clasp and gave it a proper look. I'd chosen something I thought a little girl would like. It was a metal clasp with flowers and ribbons engraved into it. She lit up into a smile as she held it.

"Did I do alright choosing this one?" I ventured, although her smile said I had.

"I've never had anything like this." Her fingers lightly stroked the surface. "Mama always said they were too expensive."

Too expensive? It had only cost a silver. Just how poor was her family? "Want to put it on?"

She nodded eagerly, only to pause. "I need a comb."

"Ahhh..." I glanced behind me, to the other bed, where Aletha's purchases were sprawled. "I think Gorgeous bought one. Help me dig."

Becca hopped off the bed willingly enough, but as she did, she asked, "Why do you call her Gorgeous, or Wifey, or Darling? And you call me sweetums, and kiddo, and Tail doesn't have a proper name either, and neither does Cloud, which I think is weird, don't you like people's names, or do you not use them 'cause we're in a dangerous place and you're afraid that people will use our names to find us, 'cause now that I think about it, that would be dangerous, and I wouldn't want people to know my name, 'cause that means they'd know where to find my family, and that would get them in trouble, but you probably thought of that, huh."

I stared at her in amazement. How had she managed to say all of that in one breath?! Didn't this girl need oxygen like everyone else? "Ah, um, well, I hardly ever call someone by their name. In my family, you see, we were only called our full names if we were in trouble or if it was something serious. We always used nicknames."

"Ohhhh." She nodded in understanding. "So it's not 'cause it's dangerous?"

"Well, it would be, because our names down here will tell people where we're from. But from now on, you're a Riic, remember."

Becca put a solemn hand over her heart. "I will."

"And Riics are famous for being in Jarrell, so anyone that tries searching for you by just your name will be going waaaay north and away from your family." Which was another bonus to me adopting her as my sister.

A knock came at the door before Aletha stuck her head in. "Since you're amiably talking, I take it that all is forgiven?"

I swiped a hand over my forehead and gave an overly dramatic sigh. "It was a close call."

Aletha laughed and came all the way into the room. "Hopefully we can avoid having to do any of that again. Now, dinner is being served downstairs. Who's hungry?"

We all raised our hands, except Tail, who had a large fish to finish off.

"Then, Becca, let's get your hair done, and we'll get something to eat."

"I want to, but I can't find the comb," Becca explained.

"Ahh...it's in that small pile of bundles somewhere." Aletha joined her at the bed and started sifting through the bags and boxes. "I bought two, just in case, as I always lose at least one comb while I travel."

Huh. Now that was funny. I always packed two whetstones for the same reason. One of them would disappear before the journey's end. It was like a universal guarantee.

Aletha found the comb in the next moment and handed it over to Becca, who promptly turned and handed it to me. I took it with a bemused frown. "You want me to do it?"

"I can't see the back of my head," she explained patiently.

Oh. Right. That would be a challenge.

For some reason, Aletha looked at the two of us with an odd expression. "Shad, how much do you know about hair?"

I blinked at her. "It tends to grow in places I don't want it to and gets tangled in weird things. Why do you ask?"

Aletha and Becca shared a speaking, very female look. "You're in for a rough time," Aletha informed my little girl with a mournful shake of the head.

"It's alright," Becca sighed, resigned. "My head's tough. I can take it."

I cocked my head at them, confused by this whole

conversation. "What?"

Shaking her head, Aletha instructed, "Start from the bottom and work your way up. Otherwise the tangles get worse."

Oh. Right, I could do that. But seriously, it was just hair. How hard could it be to draw it all up in one bunch and clip this clasp on straight?

Loggers, as a whole, were a good-natured bunch. Oh, they were notorious for being rough around the edges, and you certainly didn't want to pick a fight with them, but they weren't a bad sort. That was why I didn't think anything of dining in the main taproom downstairs. Most of the men that worked in these places were family men and not the sort to hassle women and children after all.

Out of sheer habit, I chose a table that had a ready escape route to the outside and gave me a good visual of the room. Aletha sat on one side of me, Becca on the other. We ordered something hot and filling from the serving girl that came by, sat back, and took the opportunity to unwind a bit.

Becca's head swiveled in all directions as she took in the place. As taprooms went, this one wasn't anything remarkable. Wooden beams in the ceiling, wooden floor covered in more than its share of dust, round tables and chairs clustered tightly together. We must have picked a popular place to stay, as even this late in the evening, the place was packed. We'd grabbed one of the last free tables.

When loggers got drunk, they progressively got louder, and as the beer made its rounds, the noise level in the room steadily rose. Aletha and I were more or less used to such an atmosphere, as an army barracks was rather similar in atmosphere. Becca, of course was not, and I could see her wince now and again at some of the louder yells. Not to mention the off-key singing.

I had to raise my voice to be heard over the din as I counseled her, "Ignore it and eat."

She nodded, eyes still darting about, but focused on the food as steaming plates of baked rabbit and bread pudding were put in front of us.

Ohh, the sight of the food made my mouth water. Anything was better than fish jerky at this point. A wide smile on my face, I waited for the girls to serve themselves before loading up a plate of my own.

I had half the plate consumed when I realized that Becca's attention had wandered again, this time to the table right beside ours. She had her head cocked, straining to hear what they said. The other table next to us was loud enough to drown out parts of their conversation, and even from just five feet away, I could only hear snatches. What did she find so fascinating?

Focusing, I put more effort into eavesdropping. Then I realized what they were saying and my eyes nearly crossed. Was that really the sort of thing you talked about in *public*? I was no stranger to crude words or crass conversations—I'd like to meet a soldier that wasn't—but still, there were things that you just didn't talk about in an open room like this. Especially with a child sitting behind you!

The main culprit had his back to me and was getting progressively louder as he drank. If I were being mature about it, I would have gotten out of my seat and went over to have a quiet word with him.

Naw, too much trouble.

Picking up a roll from the bread basket in the center of the table, I took aim and threw it with considerable force at the back of the idiot's head. He immediately went stiff and turned around so quickly the chair squeaked in protest. His grey eyes narrowed into slits as he growled, "What was that for?"

"Do you mind watching what you're saying in front of my little girl?" I growled back, irritated beyond belief I even had to say this.

He blinked, then his eyes went to Becca, who was staring back at him with those wide blue eyes. It was hard to tell under that swarthy skin color, but I think he reddened a bit. Then he realized Aletha was at my other side, and he really *did* blush, a faint red over his cheeks. "Missus. Miss. Your pardon."

Aletha smiled back at him, all charm. "Thank you for the consideration."

He cleared his throat, uncomfortable under her regard, and turned back around although he didn't re-engage the conversation. The whole table, in fact, became remarkably subdued.

"Shad?" Becca frowned at me slightly. "Why did you throw the bread at him?"

"Because he was talking about things that an eight-year-old should not know about," I answered frankly.

"But I don't understand what he was saying."

Thank all the gods for small favors.

When I didn't respond, she poked me with one finger in the ribs. "What did all that mean, Shad?"

I looked down at that upturned face, full of child-ish innocence, and realized that at some point in the future, I'd have to explain what that conversation meant. As well as a few other things. Ye gods, that wasn't a conversation I was looking forward to one bit.

Aletha, no doubt reading my expression well enough to guess what I was thinking, started cackling. I shot her a glare, which for some reason set her off even more, and she almost hung off the edge of the table, trying to breathe.

Some friend she was. There I was, having a crisis on my hands, and what did she do?

Laugh.

Alright, naming it a crisis might be stretching things a tad, but the thought of trying to explain the birds-and-the-bees to an innocent little girl made me squirm in my seat. It was likely a mother's job to explain all of this, but alas, Becca only had me. Which was unfair for her, true, but even more unfair for me.

It occurred to me that this wouldn't be the first time for such awkward moments. I'd likely experience this again, many times, as I ran into situations where I'd have to be mother, father, and brother to Becca all at once. How did parents do this, anyway?

Not getting what she wanted, Becca switched tactics and instead grabbed my arm, tugging insistently. "What did he *mean*?"

A parent. This feeling, these thoughts, were they what a parent would feel? I opened my mouth to respond to her but closed it again without uttering a sound. I *felt* it in that moment. When the Gardener had given me the task of protecting her throughout her life, I had taken it on as a duty, just like I'd had dozens of other duties before this one. I hadn't thought much of it, aside from what actions I needed to take and what dangers I should shield her from. But a simple bodyguard was not what I was meant to be. It wasn't what I'd offered to become to Becca, and not what she needed from me.

For a moment, an insanely clear moment, every fiber of my being understood that from this point on, Becca was *my* little girl. Not just to protect, but to cherish and guide and to teach. I would replace the father she had lost and forever be the one man that she could always depend on.

The feeling was liberating and terrifying all at once. Incredible joy had been handed to me, but it came hand in hand with responsibility so heavy I felt it down to my marrow.

How had it taken me so long to realize all of this?

Becca tugged at me again, mouth pursed in an impatient pout. "Shad."

Here I was, having a moment, and Becca was demanding an explanation of a rowdy logger's careless remarks. Chuckling softly, I gave my head a rueful shake. "Becca, I'll explain it when you're thirty."

"Why?"

"Because you're too young to know."

She paused and considered that. "You're not thirty and you know."

Aletha, trying to regain control of herself, lost it again. Or at least, she had a hand over her mouth. I wrote off any possibility of getting help from that quarter.

I matched glares with my adopted sister. "You're too smart for your own good. Eat."

"I want to know what he said," she insisted.

"Eat. Or I throw bread at you next."

Her eyes lit up. "Promise?"

That threat did not have the desired effect. I groaned. "Will you just eat?"

She let out a growl that sounded suspiciously like a sound Tail would make and reluctantly went back to her cooling dinner.

Sheesh. Kids. I thought guarding a budding Weather Mage had been quite the task, but I think raising a little girl was going to be more of a challenge.

Fortunately for all concerned, we managed to make it through dinner without any more rowdy conversations being overheard by a certain blonde and made it back to our room without further mishap. Aletha helped Becca into comfortable sleepwear and took out the hair clasp, combing her hair before settling her into bed.

I watched all my hard work being undone and almost tried for a patented Becca pout. If her hair was only going to be up for a few hours why bother making me fix it in the first place?

Even though we had a nice inn room to stay in, neither Aletha nor I was in the mood to take chances. We split up the night into two watches, and I generously let her have second watch.

Alright, fine, more like she gave me the stink eye and I volunteered myself for first watch. I did have *some* survival instincts.

The night air had a pleasantly cool, crisp feeling to it. The storm had blown away all traces of heat, and in this mountainous place, it stayed cooler anyway. I found it a nice relief from all the saturating heat we'd been travelling through. In the interest of having the best perch, I swung the window open and clambered up on the roof, sitting on the edge. The inn sat against the mountainside, up above the rest of the town, so I had the perfect vantage point. I let my legs dangle off the side and got comfortable, planning to be here for the next four hours or so.

Even as I kept my eyes peeled on the mostly deserted streets, my mind thought of other things. This whole task given to me by the Gardeners was...well, strange in a way. Protect someone, that I knew how to do. I had a lot of experience doing that. Hunt down magicians and get them out of danger before priests could find them, that I could do too. Had done so for nearly two years. But raise a little girl?

I hadn't the foggiest.

By the time I had hit my teens, the Magic War had already gathered momentum. I hadn't the time, or luxury, to think much about starting a family. Shortly after my twenty-third birthday, I'd been encased in a crystal, and stayed there for two hundred years. And when Garth got me out, well, I went straight into the next mission of rescuing magicians and trying to turn Chahir back into the country that I remembered. I'd been so busy fighting and relearning the world that I'd barely had the luxury of deciding where I'd wanted to live and make a life for myself.

Now, all of a sudden, I had a little girl to raise and little experience or knowledge of how to go about it.

I found myself to be profoundly grateful that I had to take Becca to the Isle of Strae. After all, there were people there that would be able to advise me on how to go on with this. Chatta and Garth alone would be very useful. Garth especially. I didn't know how much experience Chatta had with children, but Garth seemed to collect kids, and they all ended up adoring him after about ten minutes in his company. That had to mean he knew how to handle them.

Granted, Becca didn't seem to mind me much, and she certainly came to me first if something went wrong, but that didn't mean I always knew how to help her. That whole fiasco with me trying to untangle her knotted hair before dinner showed me that. I had a lot to learn in the parenting department.

Shadows flitting quickly across an intersection caught my attention. I leaned forward slightly, eyes narrowing as I focused. One, two...eight? Eight men in hooded cloaks? In this weather? Even late at night, it was hot enough to steam a bun.

Those *had* to be priests.

"Why, why are you stupid enough to keep wearing the hoods even when your Order is disbanded by mandate from the king?" I asked them rhetorically, shaking my head at their foolishness. "Not that it doesn't make my job easier, mind. In fact, if you simply must adhere to your fashions, don't let me stop you."

My paranoia had paid off, sadly. I'd rather have just been paranoid and gotten a good night's sleep instead of the hour nap I had after dinner. Heaving a gusty sigh, I put my hands against the edge of the roof and swung myself back into the room, landing with a loud enough thump to wake Aletha. In fact, I startled her so badly that she shot upright, hand automatically reaching for the sword leaning against the side of the bed.

"What?" she demanded around a mouth glued together with sleep.

"Priests, coming quickly this direction," I answered concisely, already throwing the packs together and reaching for Becca.

"What?" she wailed in dismay.

"We're going to get attacked, Aletha. Don't be a baby about it."

"Can we get attacked less? Is that so much to

ask?"

I didn't answer her, more focused on getting Becca. I slid my arms under her and lifted her up with a single heft. She didn't weigh much, so it didn't take a lot of effort on my part.

Like last time, she woke up the moment her body lifted off the bed and her eyes flew open. She took in the situation with a quick glance around her, then her head flopped against my shoulder in a clear gesture of frustration. "*Again*?" she asked plaintively.

"What?" I asked in mock-surprise. "You don't find ambushes in the dead of night to be fun? Where's your sense of adventure?"

She lifted her head enough to give me a glare hot enough to melt steel.

Laughing, I set her on her feet and let her get some shoes on. Tail, having nothing to pack, already had the door open and sat in the hallway, waiting on us slowpoke humans to catch up with him.

I gathered up our packs—we had sensibly left them packed before turning in—and went down first, intending to saddle the horses. If there was any mercy in the world, we could get out of this inn and away from town before the priests got here.

The way they made a beeline straight here suggested that someone had either reported us (likely) or they had some kind of device on them to detect magic (equally likely). I really hoped it was the former because that meant we could get out of here and they wouldn't be able to follow us. But even if they had a device, I still wanted out of this inn before we got into a dragged out fight. In-building fighting was one of my *least* favorite things in this world. Sword fighting in hallways was impossible, and fighting in rooms was challenging. Give me open space any day.

The girls caught up to me at the kitchen door.

"You think we can outrun them?" Aletha asked.

"I hope to," I answered honestly.

You know those large, open-spaced kitchens that professionals used to cook for businesses? The ones with plenty of counter space, middle islands, with ample walkway in between everything?

That was not this kitchen.

In fact, I'd never seen a more cluttered, cramped working space. Anyone cooking in here would have to be rail thin to fit in between the counters, and even though I wasn't particularly tall, I had to duck to keep from hitting my head against the pots hanging from the ceiling. It was a kill zone, and just stepping into the room made my skin crawl.

So, of course, that was the room that they caught us in.

I'd barely gotten halfway across the room when three of them came in through the back door, a glowing triangle device in their hands. Well, that solved that little mystery.

Shrieking *hinges*.

Here was the problem with fighting in tight, cramped quarters like this. If you pulled out a sword, you were liable to do one of two things: hit something you're not supposed to, or hit some*one* you're not supposed to. I tell you, the quickest way to lose a friend was to accidentally lob off their arm.

I'd been training and fighting with a sword for years, and I could adapt to most situations and come through them fine. But a true master understood that there were times when the sword was not the best option. That said, I could hardly go after the three in front of me barehanded. Those magicked weapons of theirs made hand-to-hand combat a bad idea.

I pulled the knife from my thigh sheath and turned sideways, settling into a proper stance that gave me room to fight and them not as much to hit.

The man in front pushed his cowl back (likely so he could see properly) and gave me a slight smile, as if trying to appear kind. "It is alright. We know that she has used her magic to charm you, to subdue you to her will. But I will break the spell for you and set you free of her."

For a moment, I was so flabbergasted that I couldn't think of a response. Then I just laughed out loud. "You expect an untrained magician to be able to *bespell* people into helping her? Wow. I haven't heard that one before. Gorgeous, you think Chatta knows a spell like that?"

Aletha snorted. "If she had, she'd have used it on Garth years ago."

"Good point."

The man frowned. Apparently we hadn't reacted the way he wanted us to. "That thing behind you is a danger to the world. Give us the girl."

I wagged a finger at him and tsked him cheerfully. "Thou shalt not have my little sister. Get this through your heads, boys."

He must have decided that nothing he said would work on us—and he was right, it wouldn't—as he simply drew two juttes from underneath the cloak.

Eyeing the weapons in his hands, I realized that for once I wasn't facing some novice trainee with little experience or combat training. He held those things like a veteran. Now, a jutte alone was little longer than a knife, and it was usually paired up with a longer sword when in combat. The fact that he drew two of them meant he'd realized what I had—sword fighting in this cramped space would not go well.

Wise of him to realize that, but I only had one knife, and fighting an experienced priest with *two* juttes would not be easy. I needed a second weapon in my hand, and I only had about two seconds to get one before he lunged at me.

There were all sorts of kitchen tools and such lying abandoned on the countertops to either side of me. My eyes took it all in within a split second. Butcher knife on my left side. Perfect. My hand reached out and snatched it up just as he threw the first attack.

He came in low, the juttes aiming for my throat and stomach. I blocked the one at my stomach and used my left hand to catch the jutte headed for my throat.

It was at that point that my eye caught sight of what exactly I was blocking with.

A ladle.

Catching the look of surprise on my face, the priest gave me a feral grin. "I think that was not the thing you wanted."

"You're right," I agreed. Even as I kicked myself for not grabbing the butcher knife, the absurdity of the situation tickled my funny bone. I was fighting a priest with a *soup ladle*, of all things.

"I'll give you a moment to switch weapons if you wish," he offered generously.

"Naw, it's fine. It's more fun this way." I meant it, too. I'd never fought with a ladle before. This should be interesting.

He clearly thought I was crazy—which I was, and he wasn't the first or last to think that—but it didn't stop him from pressing his attack. Taking a half-step in, he tried to use the jutte aimed at my throat to twist and wrench the ladle free, no doubt ending in my crushed windpipe. But the typical move wouldn't work. The spoon caught the end of the jutte and not only pulled him up short, but gave me the leverage I needed to twist and flick the jutte out of his hand.

Even as he reeled, arm flailing over his head, I slammed my elbow into his throat, then slammed the ladle into his temple. He crumpled to the ground like discarded clothes.

Hey, this thing wasn't half-bad to fight with. I twirled it in my hands like a theatrical swordsman and gave a savage grin at the other two priests. "Next!"

They visibly hesitated, looking down at the man that I had defeated with a soup ladle and then at each other. Clearly he had been the best fighter of the group, and now that he was down, they weren't really sure they wanted to take me on themselves.

"You can just quietly go away, you know," I offered kindly, tone gentle. "I won't tell, promise."

My words, sadly, had the opposite effect. They decided they couldn't let us go and so rushed me in concert. That was far from the best move. They quickly obstructed each other because of the narrowness of the aisle and tripped over their friend on the floor, so by the time they reached me, they were off-balance and in no position to give even a halfway decent strike.

Shaking my head at the sloppiness of it all, I blocked the kama with my right hand, and used the ladle to clip the other's chin. Already teetering, he didn't stand a chance. His head snapped back and he fell straight to the floor, the back of his head smashing against the corner of the counter as he fell. With a groan of pain, he came to an immediate stop on the tiles.

His friend tried to react, but I had the kama in a sturdy lock. Even as he struggled to wrestle it free, I used the handle of the ladle to slam into his sternum, which folded him over abruptly. His face was so close to my knee that I gave them a proper introduction, breaking his nose and then sending him to the ground with a grunt of pain. He lay there, gasping for breath and holding his bloodied face.

"Shad."

"Yes?"

"Did you just beat up three priests with a *ladle*?"

"I did. Wow, I'm impressive! Are you impressed? 'Cause I'm impressed."

Aletha's look at me did not convey the emotion of *impressed*. Rather the opposite, actually. "Seriously? You have a perfectly good sword strapped to your side and you pick up a ladle?"

"I was actually reaching for the butcher knife right next to it, but yes, yes I did, and you know why? Because these are tight quarters and I didn't want to risk taking someone's head off accidentally. Can I get a little thanks, here?"

For that, she poked me in the ribs. Hard.

"OWW! Can we start with you just telling me 'no' before we go to bodily harm? I'm pretty good with a no, I can work with a no."

"Will you just go? We don't know how many there are."

"One second." I leaned down and rummaged through the head priest's clothes until I found the triangle. With great satisfaction, I put it under my bootheel and stomped on it hard. It shattered in a tinkling of glass. Just in case that didn't completely do the trick, I scooped up the metal frame and put it on the counter, where I used the ladle to beat it completely out of shape. Huh. This thing came in rather handy. I eyed it thoughtfully. "Can I keep the ladle?"

Both women and the cat rolled their eyes at me.

"*Yes*," Aletha answered in exasperation. "*Go*."

Excellent.

Traveling around at midnight had its pros and cons. Mostly cons. For one, riding around on unfamiliar roads in the pitch-darkness left even me, who had a superior sense of direction, somewhat insecure about our location. Cloud and Tail both had better night vision than I did, but even they struggled with this switchback we were on. I finally called for a stop about two hours out, and we pitched a quiet camp in a small clearing. Basically, we just rolled up in our bedrolls and went to sleep, not even building a fire.

The morning sun couldn't properly penetrate through the thick canopy of leaves and branches overhead, but sunlight filtered through enough that we naturally awoke with the dawn. After only getting about four hours of sleep, I hardly felt revived and reinvigorated.

Aletha, looking as tired and worn-out as I felt, creaked to her feet. "Wakey, wakey, everyone. Time to move out."

I groaned and pulled the blanket over my head

more. I didn't care if the ground was littered with little rocks and tree branches, all of which were digging into my side. I didn't care if the morning dew was seeping into my blankets. I wanted *sleeeep.*

"Shad, that includes you."

"I'm sorry, I can't leave my blankets right now," I muttered through the cloth. "They have accepted me as one of their own, and if I leave now, our relationship will be forever ruined. I must commune with them a while longer."

"Uh-huh," she said dryly. "Becca, get him."

An exuberant child climbed onto my waist and started bouncing. I grunted under her weight and reached out a hand, snagging her and dragging her next to me. She squirmed and giggled, apparently finding this whole situation funny.

It was near impossible to sleep with a laughing, fidgety child in your bed. I gave up and threw the blanket back before rolling to my feet, deliberately 'squashing' Becca in the process. She mock-groaned in pain under my weight, laughing when I let her go again.

Why did children naturally have so much energy? And wasn't there some way to bottle it for the adults?

We had limited food supplies on us, mostly hard travel bread, jerky, and some plain water. We ate what we could for breakfast before saddling up and continuing down the trail. With the sun rising, I could gain my bearings again, and was relieved that we were more or less headed in the direction of the coastline. Aletha and I had discussed it briefly last night. If we were still getting attacked by priests this close to the Chahiran-Hainian border—and we were ridiculously close, only twenty or so miles away—then actually crossing into Hain wouldn't bring us any measure of safety. These priests were zealous in their desire to kill Becca. But she was the only living Weather Mage. It would be quite the coup if they could kill her and end a whole magical line.

But if we couldn't go west, east, or north, that only left us one option: the sea.

Our only chance at this point was to get on a boat and sail for the next safe harbor. If we could get far enough north, we'd leave behind the danger of being constantly attacked. Better still, we'd be within range of going inland to any number of magical relay stations that Vonlorisen had set up. We could call for either a ride or help if we needed to.

Of course, in order to get to that magical land of safety, we'd have to make it all the way to Movac, in Echols Province. Basically, sail halfway around the country. I didn't know if any of the small ports or fishing villages near us would either have ships going that direction or be willing to travel that far.

I might have to acquisition a boat.

As I ruminated over different possibilities and made plans for each, most of the morning slipped away. We started to smell the strong scent of the ocean, salt and water mixed together and drifting through the air. I knew we had to be close, but still couldn't see it through all the trees.

A certain group of somebodies was depending

far too much on this thick foliage to cover them and their movements. I caught glances out of the corner of my eye. Even if I had missed them, the way that Tail stared directly behind us, his ears flat against his head and his fur sticking straight up, pretty much gave them away. I had to half-turn in my saddle to see him, as he sat on Cloud's rump, but I managed it without dumping Becca from my lap in the process.

"You see 'em?" I asked him softly.

His ear twitched in my direction in affirmation.

"You get a headcount?"

Raising a paw, he delicately clawed the air three times, paused, then did it once more.

"Three you're sure of, perhaps four?"

He bobbed his head in confirmation.

"You're good at understanding him," Becca marveled.

"It was either learn quick or get scratched," I explained absently. Tail hadn't been the most patient of teachers. Now, the question was, what to do with them? I hardly wanted to go into a port and negotiate for a boat with a bunch of priests trying to take my head off.

"Gorgeous?" I called ahead.

Aletha turned in her saddle and said nonchalantly, "We've got more priests on our tail."

"So you did see 'em." I glanced over my shoulder. Where were they all *coming* from, anyway? I knew Aletha said that all the renegade priests had fled south, but surely we hadn't missed that many! I felt like we couldn't round a curve in the road without more of them coming out of the woodwork.

Well, either way, we couldn't just ignore them. I kicked a foot free of its stirrup, preparing to dismount, when Aletha cleared her throat in a meaningful way. Pausing, I glanced up. "What?"

"You fought the priests last time," she informed me primly.

"Yes, I did. Oh, are we taking turns? We are? Since when? I mean, we've never taken turns before when enemies approached, we just sort of went *yaaarrghhh* and rushed 'em."

A visible tic developed near the corner of her mouth, and I could've sworn she was trying to set me on fire with her eyes.

"Um, Aletha, my dearest, I'm sensing a little frustration from you right now. A little anger." Which worried me, as there was a distinct possibility it was *me* she was angry with, which never led to pleasant things. "Please don't glare at me so; it wounds me to my very soul. If you wish to beat up the priests until you feel better, then by all means, don't let me stop you. Stomp on them until your heart is satisfied. I won't deprive you of the pleasure."

Her glare softened—as in, it went from imminent death to a promisingly slight maiming—and she slid off her horse without a word or another glance in my direction. Pulling her sword free with a very cold *shiing*, she headed straight into the fray with the three priests without an ounce of hesitation or wariness.

Becca leaned in closer, her hands tightening into fists in my shirt. "Will she be alright?" she asked in a tremulous voice.

"There's only three of them," I assured her. Becca glanced up at me doubtfully. Oh, right, to her the priests were the ultimate boogeymen. Apparently I could be trusted to handle three at once, because to her mind, I was some sort of super soldier. But she'd not yet seen Aletha fight and so didn't know that my pretty partner was just as deadly.

Keeping an eye on Aletha (just in case), I tried to explain in terms she could understand. "For new magicians, like you, they can be dangerous and scary. But they rely on their magic too much, and they don't train as much with weapons. Not enough to really pose much threat to us, at least. That's why Aletha and I can fight them and subdue them so quickly, because they don't have enough combat training to be a match for us. Well, that and the fact that most of the priests down here were little better than novices when the whole Order disbanded. They're not fully trained, anyway."

Becca blinked at me. "What?"

"What, what?" I stared back at her, puzzled about which part had confused her.

"The Order disbanded? What's that mean?"

"The Star Order no longer exists. Vonlorisen shut it down."

"Whhhhaaat?!" she shrieked, eyes going as wide as saucers. "When?!"

"Oh, at least a year ago." Maybe more, I'd lost track of time. "Is it just me, or does Gorgeous look particularly cute when she's mad?"

Becca had to take a second to switch mental tracks, then she gave me the most befuddled look I'd seen from her yet. "Aletha? Cute?"

"Well, not when she's mad at me," I amended. "When she's mad at me, she's terrifying, but I think she's cute when she's mad and beating up bad priests. You don't think so? No? Fine, it's just me, then."

Becca gave me that patented '*Adults are strange*' look and ignored me, which for her healthy development as a child, was probably for the best.

With the priests soundly defeated and lying comatose on the ground, Aletha blew out a satisfied breath. I dared to think it safe to talk to her and ventured, "Triangle?"

"They probably have one," she agreed, as she knelt down and started rummaging through pockets. "Oooh, look! Money pouches."

"Take 'em," I ordered. We were desperately short on funds. "They owe us for the lost equipment anyway."

"A very good point." Aletha, as a mercenary, was not bothered by the idea of pilfering from enemies. It took her two bodies to find the triangle, and she beat it to death with the heel of her boot before being satisfied. "Well, that settles it: they are tracking her magic."

Becca gave me a worried look. "Does that mean you have to knock me out again?"

"Only as a truly last resort, kiddo. But no, I don't think that it would do much good in this situation. Your magic isn't flaring up, or anything. The triangles

can find even a sleeping magician." Or at least Garth's
explanation of how these things worked made me
think so. It'd been a while since he'd explained it to
me and I'd slept since then, so I might've been remembering a few things wrong.

Whether I was right or wrong, one thing was
clear: we absolutely could not stay on land.

I caught Aletha's eye. "Let's get a boat."

"And quickly," she agreed grimly, already striding
for her horse. "Oh, and Shad?"

"Yes, Gorgeous?"

"It's still my turn. You've gotten to fight with the
priests *twice*, after all."

I shook my head forlornly. "Such a stingy, greedy
woman you are."

We reached the coastline around noon, but it
took another hour of travel before we got to a sizeable
fishing village. I left the girls, Tail, and Cloud in a little
grove off the road and went into the village myself
on Aletha's horse. I didn't know what kind of rumors
might be flying about, but I didn't want to mark myself as an obvious target by riding Cloud in. A white-
haired man on a white horse was a pretty remarkable
thing after all. A white-haired man on a dark bay
horse was not.

I went about buying food and supplies with our

newly acquired funds, asking around for a boat that would take on passengers as I went. All to no avail, sadly. No one here ventured out that far, only to the nearest villages, and that was strictly for trading purposes. One person allowed that a passenger ship came by once in a while, but that usually only happened once a month and wasn't on any sort of set schedule.

We could hardly sit around waiting for a ship that might or might not show.

Which meant I had to come up with Plan B.

Now, someone in my Jaunten ancestry had been sailing before. They knew their way around boats to some degree, at least. I knew by looking at the boats at the dock what types they were, and whether or not a small crew could manage to sail them. Most of them were easily handled by a crew of two or so, which wasn't unusual for fishermen. I counted several schooners that had the right size to hold three humans, two horses, and one cat.

I meandered down to the docks and looked them over with a close eye, but all of them looked seaworthy to me. All I had to do was pick one. I hummed under my breath as I looked them over, but I didn't see anything that made me like one over the other. Finally, I went with the one that had a blue paint job.

I liked blue. Favorite color.

That decided, I turned and went back toward the village. It was difficult to kill a few hours there without raising suspicions—there wasn't much a stranger could do, after all—but I managed it somehow until the sun started setting and everyone got off their boats and went home, where dinner was likely waiting. Sitting on my haunches, well out of sight of everyone's eyes, I waited until everyone was off the docks. Then I took my packages and sauntered down the dock, up the gangplank onto my chosen ship, and set about getting her underway.

This proved to be a tad more difficult than I had planned on. Garth had warned me once that there was a wide difference between Jaunten knowledge and *experience*. He was not wrong. I almost crashed the schooner before even getting it out of the harbor.

Great guardians. I'd thought this would be fairly easy because I technically knew what to do, but I didn't have that gut feeling for the right timing on when to shift the sails, or turn the rudder, and that was the most essential part!

By some minor miracle, I managed to get around the harbor's walls and to a sheltered cove that was more or less near where I'd left the girls. Anchoring it in place, I lowered the gangplank to a rocky shore, grateful that it reached the ground. I hadn't known how we'd get Cloud aboard otherwise. Then I quickly descended and climbed back up the sloping hillside until I reached their camp.

Aletha and Becca looked up at me with absolute relief.

"Did you find a ship?" Aletha asked.

"Yes and no." Seeing her frown of confusion, I explained, "I acquisitioned a boat."

Her lips pursed in a suspicious manner. "Acquisitioned or stole?"

"Isn't that what acquisitioned means?"

My acquisitioned boat was not well-received.

Becca didn't like that I had stolen it, despite the fact we'd had little other choice in the matter. My promise to make sure it was returned (somehow) only mollified her some. What I'd actually have to do was send word to Vonlorisen—or Saroya, or someone—and explain that a reimbursement for an acquired schooner was in order. I was sure they'd take care of it. They'd covered for us in similar situations before.

The main point that neither girl seemed to be keen on was the fact we *had* a boat. Aletha had no experience with them aside from being a passenger for short jaunts. Becca knew more, being a fisherman's daughter, but she had never handled one on her own before. In fact, her experience was limited to sitting in her father's lap as he helped her steer. I was by far the most knowledgeable person on board, but I had no experience to back it up with.

When they'd learned that, they'd been less than thrilled.

Deeming it unwise to stay in the area in an acquisitioned craft, we'd drawn up the anchor and set sail, but stayed close to the coastline. I had no charts to navigate by and wouldn't know what to do with them even if I *did*. Somewhere around midnight, it got to be completely impossible to see anything, so we laid anchor again.

The next morning, Becca and I gave Aletha a crash course in rigging, steering, and sailing a schooner. Thankfully, Aletha was one of those show-once people that were a joy to work with, and she got the hang of things quickly. We set off again, making our way around the coastline.

Really, it was perfect weather to be sailing. We had clear skies, a good wind, and the temperature wasn't scorchingly hot. I sat near the aft of the ship, the wheel in my hands, idly keeping us on course. Both horses were in the lower section of the decking, neither of them particularly steady on their feet. In fact, Cloud looked rather seasick to me.

This particular schooner was only about 150 feet in length, which didn't give us a lot of room. The horses were basically crammed together in the one area big enough for them to turn around in. We humans were bunking either on the fore or aft deck, in between the rigging, as that was the only spare space to be had. As this schooner had been built for local fishing, it didn't precisely have a kitchen to it, just a potbellied stove and a bucket below decks that functioned as a sink. In fact, most of the area below decks was used as cargo hold and nothing more. It stank to high heaven, too. I didn't even want to know what had been down there last.

We all unanimously stayed up top to preserve our noses.

I sat at the helm, one hand idly steering, as Aletha puttered about at the very front of the boat, doing odd jobs. Becca clambered up to where I sat and without a by-your-leave, climbed into my lap as well.

Without any preamble, she asked, "Shad, when we get to the magic island, are we going to live in a house?"

As much as Aletha and I had explained magic to her, and where we were going, I supposed I hadn't thought to give her any details on living arrangements. Shame on me.

"Ah, no, probably not. See, the academy is one big building, bigger than a castle, and everyone lives inside of it."

"Oh." Judging by the expression on her face, she was trying to picture this in her mind but it wasn't quite making sense.

"See, a part of the academy has lots of classrooms, but there's other parts that are just apartments for the students and the teachers. I'm a teacher, but because you're my sister, you'll probably live with me."

"And Aletha," she corrected me. "And Tail."

"Tail, yes." I was confused. Why would she think Aletha...oh. Whoops. "Um, sweetums, Aletha won't be going back to Strae with us."

My little magess froze and gave me one of the best impressions of a startled deer I'd ever seen. "What?"

"Aletha came with me to help rescue you because she was worried about me going all by my lonesome, but she's a soldier from Ascalon. She'll return home after I get you to safety," I sought to explain. I mentally kicked myself for not explaining this earlier.

Becca looked at me in confusion. "But...you call her Wifey."

"I know, sweetie, I do." I scratched at the back of my head, wondering how to explain all of this to someone that had no experience with covert operations. "But we're not married."

"But you smile at her like Papa smiles at Mama," she continued, brows drawing together into a deeper frown as she spoke, "and you tease her a lot. Mama said that's a sign that a boy like a girl, and you steal hugs, and you do nice things for her without her asking, and you call her Gorgeous or Wifey or Darling, so doesn't that mean you like her?"

I had my mouth open, all ready for a rebuttal or an explanation, but that list of things rather took the wind right out of my sails. I could rationalize about half of what she'd rattled off, as some of it I was doing out of necessity for the mission in keeping our covers intact, and some of it was simply my relationship with Aletha, as we more or less used flirting as a way of communicating. But the rest of it.... I had no rationalization for the rest of it. The stealing hugs, and the smiling, and the being attentive...I didn't have to do any of that. But it felt perfectly natural to do all of it.

Those clear blue eyes were staring at me expectantly. I stared back in dawning realization that her direct view of the world had seen the heart of the matter more precisely than I had.

Had I really fallen in love with one of my dearest friends without noticing it?

"Shad?" she prompted, growing impatient.

Yes. Yes, I had. In fact, thinking about it, the only reason I'd been reluctant to leave Ascalon was that I didn't want to leave her behind. My whole mental debate about what I actually wanted was just me, afraid to own up to things. And Xiaolang, that ratfink, had been aware of it when he sent Aletha and me off on the mission. *That* was the reason for his little enigmatic smile and the *Between the two of you, you'll figure it out* line. I blew out a slow, controlled breath.

"Sweetums, do me a favor? Smack me in the back of the head as hard as you can."

Becca blinked at me. "Why?"

"It's my punishment for being an idiot."

Obligingly, she rose up a little, reeled back her hand, and slapped me in the back of the head with surprising force.

I winced at the impact but had to admit, it got my brain back in gear.

"Was that hard enough?" she inquired, a glint in her eye suggesting she wouldn't mind doing it again.

"Thanks, dearling, that was plenty hard." I gave her a repressive look, hopefully quelling any ideas she had about trying another smack without permission.

Now the question was, what to do about this? I didn't have a lot of time left with Aletha before we naturally split ways, me for Strae and her for home.

Trying to court a woman while on a semi-dangerous mission with a child in tow would surely be an interesting venture, but I'd never been one to be scared off by a challenge. Besides, in a way, we'd spent the past two years courting. I just hadn't realized it for what it was.

I wonder if Aletha would think of it the same way.

"Shad," Becca prompted, a little impatiently.

Snorting, I patted her on the head. "Well, kiddo, turns out you're not far wrong. You're not completely right, either, though."

She turned that over in her head for a moment. "What does that mean?"

"It means...we're both going to have to wait a little longer to see what the answer to that question is going to be."

I spent the next two hours trying to come up with a line of attack, but when on board a boat like this, courting resources were hard to come by. I hadn't thought up much before Aletha climbed up to where I sat and maneuvered behind me to put her chin on my shoulder, hand lingering on my shoulder blades. "How long do think it'll take to reach Movac, at this rate?"

"Three weeks," I sighed, grimacing. Strange, I only noticed now how right Becca was. We really *did* touch each other on a constant basis, didn't we? Daring to reach out, I caught up her free hand in a loose grip as I added, "And I can't imagine us managing to stay sane on board this boat for three solid weeks."

"Not to mention we don't have the food supplies for it," Aletha pointed out pragmatically. "Are you sure we can't land somewhere closer?"

"Where?" I asked helplessly. "I'm open to other options, Gorgeous. I just don't see them. There *are* no major ports before we reach Movac. It's all small fishing villages and coastal towns until we reach Echols. And Garth told me point-blank that anything farther south than Darlington was actively pro-Star Order. We saw for ourselves how right he was."

"So...Aboulmana Province...?"

"Probably as neutral as Darlington, and that's not anything to brag about. If push comes to shove, we could probably land there, but I'd rather not push our luck. We've had bad luck altogether on this trip anyway."

She groaned in agreement. "Stealing the schooner was the first thing that went *right,* and even that's a stretch. Alright, Movac. But three weeks is seriously pushing it, Shad."

"I know, I know." A long-ago event came to me, and I rubbed at my chin as I thought about it. "Gorgeous, you remember when we found Haikrysen?"

Aletha turned so that she had one hand braced against the railing with her back against it. She kept her hand in mine, though, fingers half-laced. "Yes?"

"You remember what Garth said? That it was

because Krys was actively using his magic, a bit at a time, that prevented any magical accidents from occurring."

She considered this a moment, eyes studying my face. "Are you seriously suggesting letting Becca use her magic to speed us along?"

"You're quick," I approved.

"Shad. Be serious. She's *eight years old.*"

"Nolan was fixing pregnancy issues at five," I pointed out innocently.

"That...that's really not a good example to use to support your argument." Even though she said that, she was biting her bottom lip, trying not to laugh.

"We might need to do this anyway, just to prevent a magical accident from occurring." Unease weighed like lead in my stomach. "I know she just called up that mother storm the other night, which used a lot of magic, but Chatta said there's no rhyme or reason to when magical accidents happen. They just do, whenever the mage's capacity to hold their magic hits its limit."

"And Becca's young," Aletha rubbed at the bridge of her nose, like a headache was coming on, "so her capacity to hold magic likely isn't that big. Great. I hadn't thought of that."

I sympathized. "It was a disturbing thought that woke me up this morning."

Aletha pinched her nose harder, eyes closing. "Remind me again why we didn't bring a magician with us?"

"We were in a tearing hurry to get down here?"

I offered. Honestly, if we had left any later than we had, we might not have reached Becca before the Star Order Priests did. We'd only had her a few hours before being discovered, after all. I could not regret our haste.

"So, which dangerous situation would you rather face?" Aletha asked me with false enthusiasm. "Would you rather a child mage experiment while we're on a schooner, at sea, with a power strong enough to destroy the world? Or would you rather wait until she loses control of it completely and brings in another mother storm?"

"You make those choices so enticing, my dear, I hardly know which one to choose."

She snorted. "I certainly don't know which one I prefer."

"Actually, the first option is going to be the norm, come to think of it. Remember?"

Her shoulders slumped. "Busted buckets, I'd forgotten! There's no one to teach her anyway, so she's basically going to have to figure out how to do things on her own."

"Garth and Chatta and the rest of her professors will safeguard her and advise as much as they can, but even they don't really understand how her magic works. No one living even remembers that there *were* Weather Mages."

"Except you," she amended.

"And I certainly am not an expert on it." More's the pity. "So, I vote we give her a controlled task first, let her bleed off some of that magic."

Aletha raised a reluctant hand in agreement. "Fine. I wonder, can Tail help her somehow? With his Jaunten knowledge and intelligence?"

I blinked at her. "I don't follow."

"Well, he's basically been acting as her familiar from day one." She inclined her head to indicate the two on the foredeck.

Becca, having nothing better to do, had grabbed a fishing rod and a pail and was trying to catch our lunch and augment our food stores. Tail sat on the railing at her elbow, eyes focused intently on the water. Come to think of it, those two were never very far apart from each other. In fact, more often than not, Becca was toting him around in her arms. I'd thought it was just because she was a little girl, and little girls liked to carry cats about, but...my eyes narrowed as I thought about it.

"He rather has been, hasn't he?" I regarded the two thoughtfully. "Can he be one? A familiar, I mean."

"Huh? Well, sure." I frowned at her casual response. "Hubby dearest, think about it. What's the main reason that magicians *have* familiars?"

"Hmm, to keep them on task and watch out for dangers when they're involved in a job?"

"Don't you think Tail is smart enough to do that?"

"Oh. Huh. I suppose he is at that. Which is good, as he wouldn't take it kindly if Becca tried to get another familiar. He seems to think she belongs to him." Which could explain why he and I didn't get along at times. He certainly hadn't liked it when I knocked 'his girl' out cold.

Aletha must have read as much on my face, as she gave me an evil grin. "You realize that if you knock her out again, he *will* exact revenge."

"I'm trying not to think about that, thank you," I responded with injured dignity.

She cackled, enjoying my discomfort. "Ah, that's right, I'd forgotten that the super soldier was afraid of cats."

Eh? What was she...oh. "Now wait a minute, the last time I ran from a cat it was a Life Mage in the shape of a great big *panther*. You'd run too!"

"And the reason why you're afraid of this one is...?"

"He's more cunning and evil? I don't know how he'll get his revenge, but I won't enjoy it, and I'd rather not tempt fate."

"Coward," she teased.

"I pick my battles, thank you." Wanting out of this conversation, I stood up slightly and got a look inside Becca's bucket. It seemed she had quite a catch in there. "I think she's caught enough for lunch. Call her up here. Let's see if we can give her enough information about how magic works that she can help increase our speed."

Aletha, game to try, went down and called Becca up. I aimed for a clear patch of sea that wouldn't require my constant attention and locked the wheel into place, letting the schooner just sail itself for a little while.

When Aletha came back up and saw the strap, she frowned at me and gestured me out of my chair. What, did that make her nervous? I grinned at her as we switched places and she took up steering the schooner instead.

I sat on the ground and pulled Becca toward me, settling her on my knees so I could look her more or less in the eye. "Sweetheart, I'm not a magician, but I do know *a little* of how magic works, and I think it would be better for all of us if you understood it more."

She perked right up, eyes fastened on me. "Tell me."

"First, you know the difference between a mage and a witch?" She shook her head—I wasn't surprised by her ignorance, all things considered—so I started with the bare basics. We must have sat there a good hour, me explaining everything I knew, her asking questions. Even Tail listened attentively, and he *knew* everything I knew.

Familiar, huh? Aletha was right, he certainly acted like one.

I finally reached the end of my knowledge and stopped, watching Becca. Her forehead was creased as she tried to wrap her head around everything I'd explained. Finally, she ventured, "So I don't need a wand or anything to work my magic."

"Right," I confirmed patiently.

"And my magic likes to be used."

"Right."

"And when I use it, it feels like it did that night, like there's a fire inside of me, right here." She put both hands over her heart. "And if I want to calm my magic, I try to make my chest feel cool again."

"That's how Garth explained it."

Becca's head cocked. "You've mentioned him before. Lots of times. Who's Garth?"

"Rhebengarthen, an Earth Mage from Chahir," I explained. "He's the first mage discovered in over two hundred years, so he's often called the Advent Mage. You'll meet him very soon."

Her eyes went wide. "*I* will?"

"Sure! He built the magical academy on the Isle of Strae—you know where that is? Yup, waaaay north of here. Anyway, he helped us get down here in Chahir to find you, so he knows about you, and he's researching right now all about your magic so that he can help train you."

Becca seemed a little overwhelmed by all of this.

"He's a very nice man, Becca," Aletha inputted from the side. "We worked with him for almost two years, rescuing the magicians out of Chahir. You'll find he's rather quiet, but he's charming too, and he adores children. He and his wife Chatta are very good friends of ours."

"You're *friends*?" she asked in amazement.

"Sure. Who do you think got me out of the crystal?" I grinned at her, amused at her reaction.

"Whoa." She didn't seem to know what to think about that.

What was it about Garth anyway that made him so awe-inspiring to people? Becca barely knew who he was, and she was already impressed.

"I think we got sidetracked, kiddo." Not that it

was bad she learned all of this. It would ease her worries about where we were going. "Now, what's the first rule of magic?"

"Ah...."

"It follows intent," Aletha answered promptly, lips curling up at the corners.

I applauded. "Give the girl a cookie!"

Aletha groaned. "What I wouldn't give for a cookie...."

After eating nothing but fish and bread the past two days, I had to agree with her on that one. "So, Becca, let's work a little magic. Your *intent* should be just to make more of a tailwind for us. Push the ship to go a little faster."

Her eyes nearly crossed. "NOW?!"

"Sure. Nothing to be afraid of. Just be careful, and don't knock us overboard. Tail isn't a fan of being dumped in the ocean, are you, Tail?"

The cat's ears went flat, and I could hear his evil thoughts from here.

I put a supportive hand on Becca's back. "Deep breath, honey," I advised. "You'll be fine."

She took in a deep breath, but her worried expression didn't ease. "Do I have to say something?"

"Like a magical incantation? No, not for this. There's a few spells you'll learn—I've seen Garth use them for wards—but most of the time, just imagine what you want to happen and will it to do so. That's all it takes." I thanked all magic that I had inherited my Jaunten blood from Night. He knew a lot about magic from his mother, after all.

Actually, Tail now knew everything from that magical bloodline too. Maybe him being Becca's familiar was a really good idea.

Becca took in another deep breath, but this time a hint of steel came into those blue eyes. She raised her hands, like she was trying to grasp the heavens, then she slowly lowered them. As she did, the wind started to pick up from behind us, and the sails snapped taut, the schooner picking up speed.

"Perfect!" Aletha approved. "Is it hard?"

Shaking her head, Becca smiled, although she looked a little bemused. "No. It's...easy. Like the wind *wanted* to obey me."

"It did," I assured her. "When you call to your natural element like that, it will respond readily. Just make sure to keep in mind exactly what you want."

Becca nodded soberly. I think the mother storm she'd called by accident still scared her. Maybe having her do this was good in more than one way.

"Just keep that up for a while," Aletha requested. "Don't strain yourself, though."

"Quit when you get tired," I backed her up. "But do it for as long as you can. We want to reach Movac as quickly as possible."

Becca sat quiet and still, concentrating, for quite a long time. Eventually, though, she became comfortable with it. I knew she had, because she climbed off my lap and scampered back down to the lower decks where she went to pet the horses. I blew out a covert breath of relief.

Hopefully that would deter any magical accidents.

With Becca's determined help, we made good time. Far better than what we would have managed the normal way. Cheating with magic had its advantages. Becca would take breaks, now and again, as her concentration faltered, but she kept it up steadily for hours at a time.

Without a sea chart at hand, I had to rely on my memory and landmarks to determine where we were, but within five days, we had reached Aboulmana. I estimated that at this rate, we'd make it to Echols in another two days.

Everyone agreed that the sooner we got off the schooner, the better.

The problem was there wasn't much to *do*. We could fish, and eat fish, and clean up the decks, and sleep. Oh, did I mention we could fish? After eating nothing but fish and bread, I was thoroughly sick of both. It would be a good year before I could face fish again after this.

For lack of anything better to do, I stood at the rail

with a fishing rod in my hand. Idly, I watched Becca roam around the decks. Her wind was coming in good and strong, but it no longer required her absolute concentration, and now, she would putter around doing other things while she kept the wind going. I took it as a good sign.

She meandered over to my side and peered into the bucket at my feet. "Tail is kind of tired of that fish, Shad, I think he wants to eat something different, and isn't it funny that cats can get tired of eating the same thing over and over, I thought it was just humans that did that, but apparently cats do it too, because last time I cooked it for him, he flattened his ears and stared at it for a looong time like he was trying to decide if he was going to eat it or not, and he eventually did eat it, but I don't think he really wanted to, he was just being nice about it, so I think we should try to catch him something different, do you think you can do that?"

It never ceased to amaze me that she could say all of that in one breath. At first, I was worried that she would run out of air and faint right in front of me, but it hadn't happened yet. Becca was apparently one of those people that just thought out loud. She had no filter for her mouth whatsoever. I found it completely entertaining.

"Sure," I told her, as she had paused and looked expectantly, as if waiting for an answer.

"Really?" She gave me a doubtful look, mouth pursed judiciously. "Because Aletha said you weren't really good at fishing, that you barely knew the basics, and it'd be better if I didn't ask you."

"She lies, kiddo. Lies, I tell you." I drew myself up, affronted, and shot my companion a dirty look. The schooner was too small to have a private conversation, so Aletha could hear every word we said, but she steadfastly refused to look in our direction. "I'm a master fisherman. I catch fish whenever I throw a line in."

"But you only catch *one kind*," she responded, still with that suspicious look on her face.

"Like you can control what you catch."

"You can." Now she looked at me with outright pity, as if I had said something stupid. "If you know how."

"Ho-ho, is that right?" I stared right back at her, but she didn't seem to be pulling my leg. "You think you can?"

"I can. I can even catch more than you."

"Them there's fighting words." I pointed to the other fishing rod leaning up against the side. "I hereby challenge you to a duel!"

A wicked, feline grin crossed over her face. "Loser has to clean all the fish for a *week*."

"You're on."

Normally, I slept like a dead man on a boat. Any boat. It was the rocking motion that did it, I think.

Being gently rocked back and forth was akin to being in a mother's arms again. Aletha told me once that she could do a countdown. By the time she hit five, I would be snoring loud enough to wake the dead.

It was unusual for me to wake up in the middle of the night. I went from sound asleep to looking straight up into a starry night sky. I rolled instinctively onto my side to check on Becca first. She'd snuggled in next to me a few hours before, Aletha on the other side of her. As I rolled, I saw that Aletha was waking up too, although she wasn't moving as fast I as was.

Tail sat up near Becca's head, his paw gently batting at her face, ears flat with worry. I saw why instantly. She had tears streaming down her cheeks and, soft whimpers were coming from the back of her throat.

Nightmare? I put a hand on her shoulder and shook her awake. "Becca. Sweetie. Wake up."

"Nightmare?" Aletha murmured.

"Looks like it." Not getting any results, I put an arm under Becca's shoulders and physically lifted her, jarring her out of her bedroll and directly into my lap. This snapped her awake, arms flailing a little before settling in a white-knuckle grip in my shirt. Even with her eyes open, the tears didn't stop, and she buried her face into my shoulder and kept crying. Aletha came in closer, one arm going around my shoulders, the other hand smoothing Becca's hair back from a too-flushed face, the movement steady and soothing.

I didn't ask for an explanation. I didn't need one. She'd been faced with far too much, for too long, and as a child, she didn't know how to handle it all. Becca wasn't the first magician to be forced out of her home and told to travel across the country and into the unknown. But every other magician who'd done so was a teenager. Becca was *eight*. For teenagers, it'd been risky and dangerous, and sadly, not all of them had made it. A child wouldn't stand a chance. What had her parents been thinking, sending a child off on a journey that even an adult would find hard to face?

That didn't even account for the Star Order Priests that doggedly tracked her down, time and again, trying to kill her.

She'd lost everything she ever knew in a day. She hadn't cried before this, but I didn't think it'd really sunk in until now. Or perhaps it was more that she didn't have the luxury to think about it, not with everything else that had happened. But now, she had two soldiers that had proven they could protect her from even the boogeyman himself, she was safely aboard a ship and heading for a world that would accept her with open arms, and had a dedicated furry familiar. Her new world was far from perfect, but it gave her everything she needed.

By doing so, it gave her the time to think of everything she'd lost.

"You've lost a lot, kiddo," I whispered against her hair. "It's alright to acknowledge that. Cry it all out. But don't think your family is forever lost, alright? Chahir is changing so fast, you might still be able to see them. I've seen other magicians manage it."

"R-really?" she asked around a hiccupping sob.

"Yup. Garth is a prime example. You know, he did what you're doing now—he left Chahir all on his own. He even made it to Hain without help. But after he was fully trained, he returned to his hometown and rescued his family, taking them out and bringing them to Hain."

Becca gave a giant sniff, lifting a hand to wipe at her cheeks. "You think I can too?"

"Not right now," I cautioned her. "It will work a lot better when you're fully trained, because then you can beat up those priests if they try to attack you again. But in a few years, when you're at full-strength, I'll come down with you and help move them up."

This made her pause, and she looked up at me thoughtfully. "I'll be strong enough to beat them?"

"Honey, even if *twenty* of them rushed you all at once, they wouldn't stand a chance. Not after you're trained and know how to use that power of yours properly."

Becca's mouth stretched into a feral smile that scared even me a little. "Promise?"

I held up a pinky. "Promise."

She took my pinky with her own and shook it solemnly.

"Good? Then back to sleep."

She settled back down into her blankets, the cat curling up near her chest, his head tucked under her chin. I stroked her hair gently, trying to soothe the worry away. Still, it was a long time before she fell asleep again, and even then, she frowned a little.

"Her world is so unstable right now," Aletha murmured, disturbed. "I'd thought she was taking this all a little too well."

"I think it took time for her to relax, not be on edge, before the emotions hit her." I remembered that feeling all too well. I'd felt the same after being taken out of the crystal and realizing that everything I had ever known or loved was gone, and nothing I could do would ever bring it back.

Aletha's frown deepened. "The only things permanent for her are you, and Tail, and I suppose, Cloud. Even I'm temporary. I'll return to Ascalon when this is all over."

Those words mentally tripped me up. I stared at her with growing dismay as I realized she was right. I'd been so focused on getting us all safely to Strae that I'd failed to think about what would happen after we got there. My chest constricted hard, hurting me, as I realized that I didn't want her to go.

I really, really didn't want her to go.

A man could hardly tell a woman that'd been his friend and sister-in-arms for the past two years that he wanted her to put her life and career on hold just because he'd miss her. I couldn't be that selfish. But at the same time, I didn't even want to think about the distance that would be between us once she returned to Ascalon, either.

It took me only a split second to think of what I wanted, what I needed to offer her, and the chance I was taking. In the end, I knew deep down it was worth the risk. Clearing my throat, I offered, "I, ah, don't suppose you'd reconsider?"

Aletha looked up slowly before her eyes locked with mine. "Reconsider?"

"Returning to Ascalon," I clarified, feeling like my heart was trying to beat its way out of my chest. "See, I'd really miss you. I mean, *really* miss you. Life without you would be totally boring. And I'm not just saying all of this because I want you to help me teach weapons at Strae, although really, I don't even want to try to teach a school full of kids the basics of combat by myself, that would just be dangerous in a not fun way, and you're one of the most qualified instructors I've ever seen—"

"You're babbling," she pointed out. Aletha's lips parted in a hopeful way, her eyes locked onto my face, reading every nuance.

I made myself stop. "I blame Becca. She's a corruptive influence. So, um, in essence, I want you to stay with me. Us. Since Becca's a package deal, I suppose I should say us."

"Shad." Her tongue flicked out to wet her lips. "Are you proposing?"

"Over a sleeping child that just had a nightmare. Yes, yes, I am. Sorry, I have no sense of romance or timing, do I?"

"Not in the slightest." Aletha braced a hand against the deck and leaned over Becca enough to snag me around the neck and pull me toward her. I went willingly, meeting her halfway in a sweet, lingering kiss.

Ahh. Perfect. Why hadn't I done this *sooner*?

She broke the kiss and whispered against my

mouth, "I agree."

I blinked at her stupidly. "You *do*?"

"Why are you surprised?" A low, soft chuckle flowed from her. "Haven't I always dived into danger with you? Why did you think I followed you, every time, hmmm?"

Because she was as crazy as I was? No, I'd better not say that. I had better sense than to say that when she was within arm's reach of me. That was the sort of thing you told a woman with a *castle* between you, with battlements and walls and magical wards to keep you protected. I went with the safer response. "You know, you're right."

"I just have one condition." She held up a finger, that smirk of hers widening. "*You* get to hand in our resignations to Xiaolang. And explain why we're resigning."

I shrugged ruefully. "Knowing him, he's already expecting this. What that man knows and keeps to himself would fill volumes."

Aletha splayed a palm in acknowledgement. "Likely true."

"I'll buy you a ring when we reach Movac," I promised.

"And we'll tell Becca in the morning we're engaged," she added on thoughtfully. "I think that will give her more of a sense of stability, if she knows that I'm staying with all of you. It's just as well I am—you have no idea how to raise a little girl."

Considering how many things the both of them had taught me, I really couldn't argue with that. "Gorgeous, one question."

She cocked an eyebrow at me. "What?"

"I don't think you will, 'cause you don't strike me as one, but do you want one of those huge, elaborate weddings like Chatta and Garth did?"

"No," she responded adamantly, shaking her head over and over. "Oh, no, I hate formality of any sort. Why, do you?"

"Since when have I liked that sort of thing?"

"Well, you enjoyed their wedding. And Asla and Xiaolang's."

"To be precise, I enjoyed the party *afterwards*. I could have happily skipped the ceremony."

Aletha rubbed at her bottom lip in a thoughtful way. "Well, if you don't want a formal wedding, and I don't want a formal wedding, then why don't we just get married in Movac?"

"And have a party with everyone when we get back to Strae? I see absolutely no downsides to this plan."

Unexpectedly, Aletha started laughing, although she was trying to keep quiet.

"What?" I asked in confusion.

"No, sorry, I just remembered what you said before we left Ascalon. You proposed to me then too. Who would have thought pretense would become real?"

I'd almost forgotten I said that. "Xiaolang did," I answered dryly.

"Oh, yesss...." Her eyes went blind as she remembered. "He did, didn't he? Remind me to do something to him for being so smug and mysterious."

I gave her a salute. "I will. And I insist on helping. But back to the question: you're good with getting married in Movac?"

"Sure, I am. You understand that we'll be in loads of trouble if we do that? Chatta alone will skin both of us."

I waved this away. "I live in a state of constant danger. Most of it self-inflicted."

"Which means I'm certifiably crazy for marrying you." Aletha's grin said she didn't mind that. "Well, at least life with you will never be boring."

I winked at her. "I can safely promise you that."

We told Becca over breakfast about the engage-
ment, and she was completely thrilled, and also relieved that Aletha would forever be with us. A worried
line of tension I hadn't realized was there faded out
of her body language. The rest of the day, and most
of the next, all I heard those two talk about was weddings and what their new home would be like.

Aletha was right, Becca had needed the extra reassurance.

I watched them chatter away and smiled, enjoying the show. I also found it enlightening. Who knew
that women cared so much about the little details that
went with weddings? Even my Aletha, who had told
me not twelve hours before that she didn't care for
ceremonies, still wanted to wear a nice dress and be
married properly in a church.

As they talked, I made mental notes. I did not
want to say something stupid later and have *two*
women mad at me.

These conversations whiled the time away, and

before any one of us really realized it, we had arrived in Movac.

Movac was one of two major seaports for eastern Chahir, and it could, by no means, be described as *small.* There were so many ships coming and going out of the harbor that I felt like I was playing some aquatic version of dodgeball with the schooner, trying to miss people. Usually there was some rhyme or reason for coming in and out of a harbor, but if this port had a system, I certainly couldn't figure it out. Every size of ship from rowboats to three-tier passenger ships could be seen, and Becca went from one side of the schooner to the other, exclaiming over them.

Someone had had the good sense to put up signs at the ends of the docks that stated the terms of docking and fees involved. We had to sail about halfway down, more towards the center of the moon-shaped harbor, but we finally found a dock that would let anyone in for a minimal fee. I had a feeling that the small fee meant a distinct lack in security, but as we had no intention of coming back to the schooner or leaving anything behind, I frankly didn't care what happened to it.

In great relief, we put the gangplank out, threw all our gear onto the horses, and clattered toward land. Cloud kept rubbing up against my side in thanks, grateful to have solid land under him. (It was going to be reaaaaal fun convincing him to board a ship again.)

A wizened old man with a potbelly sat at the very top of the dock with a large ledger in front of him. I assumed him to be the master and stopped in front of him, offering a polite bow. "Riicshaden. A pleasure to exchange names."

"Entgarderen, pleasure. That schooner with the blue trimming yours?"

"That's right," I responded easily. "She won't be here long, as a friend of ours will be picking her up." Whether to sell her or somehow send her back, I did not know, nor did I care. "What's the fee for her?"

"How long will you keep her here?" he asked, clearing his throat.

"Two days?" I offered. Surely I could sort the problem of the schooner out by then.

We haggled out a price that I thought more or less fair, and I paid him before asking, "If we were to buy tickets for a passenger ship heading toward Halliburton, where would be the best place to go?"

He dipped his chin a fraction and eyed the group thoughtfully. "You got traveling papers?"

I stared at him in dawning realization. Oh. Oh, busted *buckets*. I'd forgotten about those! I was so used to Garth zipping us all over creation, avoiding border checks and roads altogether, that I'd forgotten Chahir had instigated a mandate that anyone traveling out of one province and into another had to have official papers. Of course, Vonlorisen had decreed that to try and capture the renegade priests, but...shrieking hinges!

I didn't have papers for Becca!

Aletha stepped around me and offered the man a resigned shrug. "My husband and I do—" we did, too, we'd automatically packed them with the rest of our gear before leaving Ascalon "—but I'm afraid we lost our daughter's over a week ago. It's been a rough trip."

"You folks look a mite rough," he agreed. "Well, you'll need to go to the main government office and get another set made. Don't envy you that, it's a right chore."

"Where might that be?" Aletha asked him.

He gave us directions, which I more or less followed as I was familiar with Movac. I repeated it back to him to make sure I had it straight, thanked him for the trouble, and led the group off toward the main part of the city. "Well, I suppose we have to go find an inn first," I told Aletha as we navigated our way through the cramped streets. Where did all these people *come* from, anyway?

She dodged a draft wagon coming our direction, automatically shifting Becca closer to me so that she was out of harm's way, before answering, "We'll need to, just to put our gear somewhere and stable the horses for a while. I get the feeling that getting those papers for Becca will take a few hours, at least."

I gave her a smile known to melt women's hearts and charm birds into singing. "My darling, why don't you do the paperwork for Becca? I'll hunt down passenger ships and give us some options to choose from."

Aletha smiled at me winsomely. "I think not."

Hmm. My legendary charm had mysteriously failed.

Alright, time to go to Plan B.

I wrapped my arms around Aletha's shoulders

and in my best pitiful tone whined, "But I'm terrible with paperwork! Aren't women supposed to be naturally better with it?"

She tried to act put-upon, but I could tell she was biting back a smile. "Shad..."

Between us, Becca was giggling at my antics, which, of course, only encouraged me.

"Please? Pretty please? I'll buy you a nice bribe later, I promise."

"Shad," she repeated patiently, turning her head slightly to look me in the eye. "I can't read or write Chahiran, remember? I only know how to speak it."

I opened my mouth, all ready to protest, and froze when I realized what she had said. "Busted *buckets.*"

"So unless you want an eight-year-old to fill out all that paperwork—and I wouldn't recommend that—you're stuck."

I was having the absolute *worst* luck on this trip.

We found an inn without issue, a pleasantly clean place with friendly staff that was near the waterfront. It was barely nine in the morning, so we had plenty of time left in the day to do things, so we unanimously decided to clean up first. None of us had had a proper bath in days, after all.

The staff gave us directions to not only the office I needed to visit for Becca's traveling papers, but also to the main ticketing office for passenger ships, both of which were on the same street. Actually, they were within spitting distance of each other. Since that was the case, we went together, weaving our way in and out of the foot traffic until we reached the center square of the city where most of the main offices were.

I picked out a café on the corner for us to meet up at, girded my mental loins for battle, and waded into the building.

Of course, it was a useless gesture on my part as all I did was join a line of shuffling people and stay there for the next hour.

The building, at least, was cool. It had been built during the turn of the century (the massive spider webs in the corners led me to believe so), with thick granite walls and wooden beams supporting a sturdy tile roof. Sound echoed in here, as the main room took up half the building. People were crammed together in one line of desks dividing the employees from the patrons, but in spite of the vast number of people in this one space, it wasn't particularly noisy. Oh, people moved about, and chairs scraped on the tile floor now and again, but there was nothing more than a quiet hum of conversation as people went about their business.

What a dreary place to work in.

When my turn finally came, I went directly to the desk an usher waved me to without much thought on my part. I thought, no matter how much time this supposedly took, it couldn't be *that* bad if there was someone to help you with the forms, right?

Where was Eagle when I needed him?

Here I sat in front of this crotchety old soul, who looked to have been born in that chair. He creaked when he moved, wrinkles making him seem like he was permanently frowning, hair wispy and standing straight up. He prattled on about what I needed to do, and what forms, and what forms I would need to fill out other forms, and so on.

The problem was, I didn't understand a word he was saying.

I didn't know what language he was speaking, but it wasn't Chahirese. Or Hainish. Or Solish. Or any other language I happened to know. I was pretty sure it was some bureaucratic dialect that only government officials spoke.

Two years ago, when I'd been pulled out of the crystal and told what the mission was, I'd had no problem helping to rescue magicians out of Chahir. We'd gone over the border as we pleased, back and forth, without any issue. I didn't even remember being stopped unless we were heading into a major city and going through the main gates. And that was when the world was actually *dangerous* compared to now, when the Star Order was still in charge of things.

So explain to me, when we were relatively safe and sound, why did we suddenly have all these bureaucratic safeguards to wade through?

I tried to tell myself that this was a good sign. That all these checkpoints and countermeasures showed that Vonlorisen was taking the security of his country very seriously. But as another form was shoved into my hands, the argument fell a little flat.

He beamed at me.

I blinked back. "Is that it?"

"Yes, sir, that's all. Simply fill these out and return them to me."

I stared at the thick wad in my hands and suddenly missed the days when I could just go around hacking at people. Life was simpler then. "Right." Still not sure how I got stuck with all of this, I pushed myself out of my chair, banging my knees against the short desk in front of me in the process. Grimacing, I cursed under my breath and hobbled over to a set of tables behind me.

Obviously the people who worked here realized that their patrons needed a place to sit and write, as they had a whole line of tables shoved together against one wall. I took a chair across from an old woman who was hunched over her own pile of forms, and I started with the first one in front of me.

The names of the applicants, and their birthplace and such, all of that I knew. But about three lines into the form, I quickly became stuck. Becca's date of birth? I had no idea. I barely knew her age. Her parents? Siblings, if any?

Ahhh...I scratched at the back of my head. Well, technically we weren't supposed to tell who she was, as we were trying to avoid getting her family in trouble. So I supposed here, I should say *my* parents? And sibling would be me, right? I scribbled in answers, skipping whatever I didn't know.

I got through three of these obnoxious forms

when it hit me: we were in Echols Province.

Each province was like a city-state of their own. They might've all been under Vonlorisen's rule, but they all had their own legal systems. It had been a nightmare for us when we were tasked with ferreting out the Star Order Priests, as we'd had to deal with different judicial systems, all of which were different, none of which talked to each other across the provincial borders. It had taken a direct order from Vonlorisen to get us through the systems and give us the power we needed to hunt down and imprison the priests.

But now, the holes in the system might just work in my favor.

I was in *Echols*. Echols did not share information with any other province, and certainly not with Kaczorek, where Becca was from. They wouldn't cross-reference my information with Jarrell Province either, and even if someone was willing to go hunt everything down and compare my answers, it would take *months*. They promised at the front desk that as long as I filled out all the necessary forms, I could have a passport for Becca today.

So, really, it didn't matter what I put down as long as it seemed logical on the surface.

An evil grin stretched from ear to ear. Oh. Oh, this would be *fun*.

Humming under my breath, I started in again, but this time I put down whatever I wanted to. I made up whole families, birthdates, occupations, and so on. The only thing I checked was to make sure that my lies were consistent and that I never contradicted myself.

Pleased with myself, I went back to the crotchety man and handed him the forms.

He took them, eyes peering up at me over the rim of his glasses. "You were quite fast."

"You were very good at explaining them to me," I responded kindly.

His mouth dropped open. Had he never been complimented on the job before? Embarrassed, he cleared his throat, nodding for me to take a seat, and started going through the forms. Almost instantly, he frowned. "These are out of order."

"Oh, are they? I'm so sorry." There'd been an order?

Still frowning, he shifted them about in his hands, putting them into whatever order he wanted, then he started again from the top.

Perhaps because he'd been doing this job for the past hundred years he knew how to read through the forms quickly. He went through that stack with record speed then lightly tapped them against the desktop, knocking them into perfect alignment. "Well, these seem to be in order. I'll stamp them and bring back the proper documentation."

I let out a covert breath of relief.

Halfway out of the chair, he paused. "How is it that you have your own documents and passports but not your sister's?"

Ahhh...*cripes*, did he have to think of that? I gave him a half-truth. "We were hit by a mother storm about a week back. It basically destroyed most of our traveling gear and such. I had mine in my belt pouch, so that was safe, but her bag was lost."

His mouth formed an 'ah' of understanding. "Poor luck."

I grimaced in agreement. "We've had nothing but bad luck this entire trip."

"Hopefully that doesn't continue," he offered. Was that a smile, however fleeting?

Strangely, I'd felt like I'd made a friend, and I grinned back at him. "Hopefully not."

He turned and went off to a back room, coming back within minutes with some very official looking papers in his hands. Sitting back down, he filled them in with a quick, neat penmanship, stamped them several times with all sorts of seals, and then handed them to me. "Good journey, Riicshaden."

"Thank you…I never did catch your name?"

He looked at me with wide eyes, expression touched. "Corsamen."

"Corsamen, a pleasure to exchange names. And thank you for your help."

He almost looked on the verge of tears. Seriously, had *no one* ever thanked the man? Or were they too irritable to do so after wading through all of those obnoxious forms?

"Safe journey," he wished me again, huskily.

"Thank you." I gave him a casual salute before gathering up my papers and heading back out of the building.

Both girls were waiting at the café on the corner. They'd clearly been waiting on me for a while, as there were all sorts of dishes stacked up. Well, someone'd been enjoying themselves. Becca spotted me first and waved. "Did you get it?"

"I did," I assured her, slinging myself into the chair nearby. "How long was I in there?"

"Three hours," Aletha answered dryly. "How many forms were there?"

"I swear, you can buy a house and do less paperwork." I waved the passport and boarding pass in the air. "It was tricky, too, as I didn't know half the things they were asking me."

"So what'd you do?" Becca asked.

"I lied," I answered cheerfully. "No one's going to check to see if I told the truth, not when we're in a province so far from your hometown."

"You lied," Aletha repeated in amusement, "on official paperwork, and got by with it?"

"Hey, my charm is not to be discounted."

She snorted. "Shad, you're a bad man."

"I couldn't have told the full truth anyway, even if I'd known all of it," I pointed out to her. "The possibility is remote, but what if someone put the pieces together and connects Becca back to her family? It would put them in danger."

Her open hand conceded the point. "There really wasn't another option, I suppose. Well, we have a boarding pass and passport for her. What else?"

"Traveling clothes? What we've got on is worn out. Did you buy us tickets?"

"Turns out there's only one ship leaving for Halliburton this week, and it goes out tomorrow morning," Aletha answered. "So yes, I got one of the last rooms available."

"That doesn't give us a lot of time," I responnvded with a frown. "Do we have time to get married today?"

A twinkle appeared in Aletha's eye. "No, but apparently if you tell the ship ahead of time, the captain performs wedding ceremonies. In fact, they even give you a honeymoon discount if you're married on board."

I blinked at her. "Now how in the world did you learn about *that?*"

"It pays to talk to people while you're standing around in line, it truly does."

"So is there anything we need to do?" This recent stint of doing paperwork had made me hyperaware of it.

"I've already done it. Well, actually, they helped me fill it all in."

Bless the guardians for small favors. "Excellent. Since the ship doesn't leave until tomorrow morning, we have time to do some shopping."

Becca perked up at this idea, as girls normally did when shopping was offered. "Can I buy a pretty blue dress?"

"I insist you do," I told her in grand, rolling tones.

She hopped out of her chair and into my lap, hugging me around the shoulders. "You're the best big brother *ever.*"

"Awww, that'd be sweet if you meant it, but you're only saying that because I spoil you rotten."

Pulling back, she blinked at me innocently. "Is that bad?"

"Not for you," Aletha said dryly. "Alright, shopping it is."

Movac, as it turned out, was an excellent place to go shopping.

Because of its location, it saw a lot of trading with Bromany, Q'atal, and even Hain. It was *the* port to send things to if you were shipping things overseas. Once we'd left the more formal, government section of the city and reached the marketplace, it was immediately obvious that we wouldn't get a second glance here. I'd never seen such a mix of foreigners in my lifetime, not within Chahir's borders, at least.

Just as obvious, it was rush hour. People were packed into the streets like sewer rats. The signs were way above eye level, no doubt because the merchants realized that you could walk right past their store and not notice it was there during the rush hour. Thankfully we were in a fairly modern and clean city. Otherwise, in this press of bodies, it would have quickly stunk to high heaven.

I kept a watchful eye on a certain small blonde as she and Aletha headed for the first clothing merchant they saw. As they browsed, I went through the store and bought a few things for myself, bundling it all up into a more cartable load. While I'd had my back turned, Becca had somehow managed to find five dresses, three pairs of shoes, and I didn't know how many hair ribbons that she just *loved* and *can't I have all of them*?

So, of course, I bought everything she wanted. My purse winced when I did, but it didn't stop me. Seeing the first honest smile on her face more or less bewitched me, and I just gave into her without even trying to argue. If buying her this made her forget—for at least a moment, everything she had lost—then it was well worth it.

Aletha watched me do this and shook her head, resigned. I think she realized at that point I'd be the fun parent and she'd be the disciplinarian.

We went from that store to the next, where Becca insisted we had to buy something for Tail too. The store mostly had pretty, shiny things and baubles, things more suitable for courting gifts. Aletha chose to go to a shop a little further down, as she wanted new traveling bags to put our purchases into.

So I dutifully kept one eye on Becca as I bent over the wares on display, hoping to find a good set of wedding rings for Aletha and me as we shopped. I kept an eye out for something that might suit an evil Jaunten cat too, but nothing spoke to me.

"Becca, I think we need to change stores," I said at last. "I don't see anything here that—" Huh? Wait a minute, where did she go? She'd been right at my side a moment ago. "Becca?"

I turned and went outside the store, but still didn't see her. Growing concerned, I raised my voice. "Becca! Becca, where are you?"

No answer. Or at least I didn't hear an answer. The marketplace was noisy, but surely not noisy enough to crowd out a screaming child.

Right?

Unless...Aletha and I both had seen signs that this city had mostly accepted magic, so we'd relaxed our guard, but what if there were still priests here? What if they had seen Becca, recognized her for what she was, and kidnapped her?

Frantic now, I started shoving people aside, calling out in the loudest voice I could muster. People dodged me as I roughly went past them, looking at me with either annoyance or pity, but no one offered to help.

"Shad!"

Aletha? I spun about sharply, heading to where I had heard her voice. It took several eternal seconds, but I finally managed to break through to where she stood, resting in the corner of a shop's awning.

Aletha had her arms crossed over her chest, toe tapping an irritated rhythm, a visible tick at the corner of her mouth. At her side was Becca, who looked entirely innocent, even though *she* was the one that had disappeared on me and set off a minor heart attack.

"Shad," Aletha asked me in a warning tone, "where were you?"

"Looking for her," I defended myself, pointing at

Becca. "Where were you, you rascal?"

Becca looked up with sorrowful eyes. "I got lost and couldn't find you."

"Shad. Were you holding her hand properly?" Aletha demanded.

It was strange. I'd known and worked with this woman for nigh on two years now. I'd seen her in a variety of moods, from good to bad, but never once had she ever struck me as having a maternal side. But she certainly was in a mothering mood now! I'd somehow struck a chord in her, one of maternal outrage no less, and she was visibly displeased with me.

Wait, what? "Hold hands?"

Aletha let out a breath that was half growl. "Seriously, what were the Gardeners thinking? You might be the perfect man to protect her, but you have no idea how to *raise* her. Yes, Shad, you have to hold hands with children in big, crowded places like this; otherwise you risk getting separated from them. Like now."

"Oh." Whoops. Did they, by chance, write instruction manuals on how to raise kids? I had a feeling I'd need one. On second thought, "How do you know all this, anyway?"

"I have younger siblings."

So did I! Although, come to think of it, my mother had never trusted me to look after them for any length of time.

Aletha let out a breath that sounded more like a rumble than a sigh. "Alright, soldier, watch and learn. Becca, let's continue our shopping." She held out a hand.

Becca took it promptly, like it was the most natural thing in the world. Me? Well, I shouldered our bags and tagged along at their heels, observing Aletha's parenting skills as ordered. I had to admit, she certainly knew more than I did. Not once did she lose track of Becca, and she even saw things about her that I didn't, like how her new shoes were giving her blisters.

Maybe Aletha would write me a parenting guide....

After three hours or so, we'd bought everything that needed to be bought and returned to the inn. We were allowed to board our ship tomorrow morning, so we chose to stay at the inn we'd first found. Aletha dumped everything on the bed and went for an early bath before dinner. She'd claimed she'd worked up a sweat while shopping. I think it was more the chance to relax in a hot tub of water and unwind a little after a disastrously stressful trip.

Either way, I didn't argue, just shooed her along. Becca and I unwrapped all our packages and repacked them into the new traveling bags.

"Shad, I'm hungry, isn't it time for dinner yet, I know that we just ate a few hours ago, but Tail's hungry and my stomach is making noises, and I don't think we want to eat anything here at the inn 'cause the smells coming from the kitchen are a little funny, they make Tail's nose twitch, not in a good way, and I don't like them either, so I think we should get something to eat, but I want to go somewhere else, like that place we passed coming here, the one that smelled yummy."

I listened to this patiently, waiting for her to run down. "Well, kiddo, I don't see why we can't go out and grab something." I had to agree with her assessment of the smells coming from the kitchen. They did not induce any mouthwatering. "That yummy smelling place we passed, you mean the outside street stall selling fried meat pies?"

"No, the *other* one," she said impatiently.

Really? That had been the one to grab my attention. I racked my brain a moment, trying to think of some other place we'd passed. "The one selling ham steaks and turkey legs and fresh rolls?"

She nodded vigorously. "That one."

"Right. Well, let's dart out real quick and get something to eat, then." Aletha had just gone down to the bath, and I didn't expect her to come back up for a good hour, at least. "We'll pick something up for Gorgeous while we're at it."

Pleased to get her way, she skipped out of the room and down the stairs to the sidewalk outside. Then she paused and turned back to me, offering a hand. "It's dangerous if we don't hold hands."

For her or for me? I decided it could go either way. I meekly accepted the hand and held it as we braved the street.

We were in that odd hour of the afternoon that left most restaurants of all sorts dead. It was too late for lunch, almost too early for dinner, so we had the place more or less to ourselves. Becca stood on her toes to see the menu, written in chalk on a blackboard nailed to the wall behind the counter. I leaned against the aged wood of the counter and watched her in amusement as she and Tail had a serious discussion about what the other one wanted to eat.

I think the master behind the counter—who had all the earmarks of being a father himself—found the scene amusing, as he also leaned against the counter and watched the conversation play out. I think he thought it was just a little girl playing pretend with a smart cat.

He had no idea it was a mage-in-training speaking with her familiar.

Finally, Becca and Tail turned to me. "We want a chicken leg, one roll, and the seaweed soup."

I assumed the chicken leg was mostly for Tail. "Master, if you would? And add another two chicken legs, three rolls, another bowl of the seaweed soup, and one more of the clam chowder."

"Right-o," he agreed amiably before turning and hollering the order to the cooks in the back. Then he turned back to me. "Master, it'll be four coppers in all and a few minutes' wait."

I dug out my wallet and rummaged for the right amount of coin. "We don't mind the wait, as long as it's fresh."

"Always is," he assured me. "I get my supplies

straight from the fishermen and farmers outside the city. Most folks from up north, like yourself, usually order the fried fish though."

I supposed my accent was a dead giveaway to my birthplace. "Well, I've had nothing but fish for the past week and a half, you see, so I'm rather ti—"

"SHAD!!!"

My first, instinctive reaction was to look down at my side, where Becca *should* have been. But of course she wasn't.

I whirled around, following my ears to figure out where Becca was. She wasn't far from me, barely ten feet away, her back to a brick wall. Tail was not in her hands, but I couldn't see enough of her through the crowd of people and the two food stalls between us to figure out what was going on.

In sheer instinct, I ran toward her, pushing people roughly out of the way. I rounded the last stand and was abruptly checked by another person, who met my advance with his own, shoving me back.

"Sir, step back—" the man tried to say.

It didn't penetrate. I could hear Becca crying, calling to me, and Tail snarling and hissing in warning. The only thing I could focus on was getting to them.

I threw a fist into his stomach, hard, folding him over. His free arm I took and twisted behind his back at such an angle that it threw him, spinning him in the air almost a full circle before he landed face-first on the ground.

Of course, the moment that I showed resistance, two more men came to block me, drawing weapons as they did so. It was only then that I realized these weren't priests—in fact, they wore uniforms that proclaimed them as local city guards.

What?

City guards? Now, that changed the game here. Blinking in confusion, I took a half-step to the side, trying to figure out how many I was up against. Four? No, there was another one trying to get around Tail. Ha! Wished him luck on that.

"Becca," I called to her in a voice that carried over the street noise. "Stay right there, don't panic. I don't think you're in danger, it's just a little mix-up."

She had both arms around her chest, eyes wide with terror. Her hair was starting to swirl around her shoulders a little, despite the fact that there was no wind here. Even without a magician's eyes, I could tell her magic was starting to rise, reacting to her panic. Her mouth opened, closed, eyes darting to the armored men around her. "B-but—"

I looked at her steadily. "Becca." She didn't look at me, too wrapped up in fear, and I sharpened my tone to get her attention. "*Becca*. Trust me. Don't move."

For a long moment, she searched my eyes, but the wind gradually died down. I wasn't panicked or worried, she saw that, and it gave her the courage to rein in her magic. Giving me a jerky nod, she sank and gathered Tail up in her arms, clutching him with a hold tight enough to leave bruises. The cat didn't seem to mind, as he was busy spitting and hissing at anyone foolhardy enough to get close.

"Sir," one of the two facing me said in warning,

"you are assaulting Movac City Guardsmen and—"

"*You*," I cut him off icily, "are scaring my little sister. Now, what business do you have with us?"

"Sir—" he tried again, "—we are under orders to—"

"Your superior officer," I cut in again, recognizing from his tone that he was going to give me that official statement garbage. "Where is your superior officer?"

"Right here." An older man with white hair at his temples and a greying beard stepped around his men. He looked to be in his early fifties or so, hardened with experience, but with the eyes of someone who didn't just blindly follow orders. "Sir, you might be unaware that your sister is a magician?"

"Weather Mage, to be precise," I answered calmly. Ahhh, I bet I knew what was going on here. "I assume that you have a triangle or something that told you what she is, and came to collect her and send her to Strae Academy on Vonlorisen's orders?"

The man blinked. "You know what she is? And what our orders are?"

Oh did I ever. "Sir, my name is Riicshaden, Professor of Weapons at Strae Academy." Although I hadn't assumed that position yet. Details, minor details.

His eyes bugged out so far they nearly fell out of his head. "Professor of Weapons, you say?!"

One of the men to my right muttered to his companion, "Wasn't Riicshaden the name of the man that helped clean the Star Order out of the country?"

"That's me," I confirmed, not looking in their direction. It was more fun to watch the officer in front of me splutter, completely taken aback by my identity. "Now, gentlemen, let me re-introduce you. This is my sister, Riicbeccaan, a Weather Mage. I'm her legal guardian. We're on our way to Strae Academy. Is there a problem?"

The officer snapped into attention. "Sir! I'm Guyroben, Captain of the Movac City Guard First Division. We apologize for the confusion. We assumed the girl was an unknown magician and needed protection."

I held up both hands. "Understood. I know exactly what your orders are. I'm the one that wrote them, you see."

Quite a few of them choked hearing that.

Ignoring them for a moment, I crouched down and held out my arms to Becca. She flew into them without a second of hesitation, one hand clutching Tail to her chest, the other arm around my neck. I thanked all magic that Tail was sentient, as any other cat in that position would have been clawing his way to freedom right about now.

"Professor Riicshaden," Guyroben said respectfully, "we sincerely regret scaring your, ah, sister. A Weather Mage, you say?"

I nodded confirmation, but I was focused on Becca. "Becca, these men aren't enemies. Actually, quite the opposite."

She looked up at me doubtfully.

I sighed internally. Right, that didn't sound convincing when six armed adults surrounded you. "See, they're used to magicians being in trouble, bad trouble like I found you in, so they snatch up the magicians first and then apologize later. They're less likely to have casualties that way."

Her brows beetled as she considered that. Then she peeked at Guyroben. "So he's not a bad man?"

"Not at all," Guyroben assured her gently. "I'm under orders from the king to protect any magician I find. In fact, I have a nephew who's a wizard and is at Strae Academy right now. I didn't know they had a Weapons Professor, though." He looked up at me with consideration, as if now wondering if I'd sold him a line.

"It's a new position, actually, and I haven't taken it up yet," I explained patiently. "I'll do so when I return with her."

"Ah. I'd wondered."

"At any rate, they're not bad men," I assured her firmly. "They just didn't know you already *had* a guardian to protect you. So do me a favor? No calling in storms 'cause you're scared?"

"I'll try not to," she promised faithfully. Since she had color returning to her skin, and her death grip on me and the cat had eased, I assumed her panic had passed.

"Good girl." I turned and looked down at the man I'd thrown, who was groaning his way up to his feet, a hand held protectively over his stomach. "Sorry for that, by the way."

The man had enough grit to look up at me and give a strained smile. "I certainly know why you were offered the position of Weapons Professor, sir. No worries, I won't take offense at this."

"Perhaps this will teach all of you to ask questions first?" Guyroben asked his men dryly. "Professor, is there any assistance that we can offer you?"

"Now where were you earlier today, when I had to do all sorts of bothersome paperwork to get us passage on a ship?" I asked him wryly.

He shrugged, lips kicked up on one side. "You still would have had to do the paperwork. Trust me on that."

Ah well, that figured. "Do you have a way to send messages directly to Strae?"

"We do," he confirmed.

"Excellent. I need to send one to Garth, let him know we have Becca and we're on our way back. I'm afraid he might have lost us down there, even if he was keeping track with a pool."

Guyroben studied my face intently. "By Garth, you wouldn't happen to mean Magus Rhebengarthen?"

"That's him." I waited to see his reaction.

The man merely swallowed, hard, but otherwise kept his composure admirably intact. "I see. Professor, if you'll follow me, I'll escort you so you can send that message. If you can, tell me the full events of how you managed to retrieve your sister as we walk. For the sake of my report, you understand."

Report, my left foot. I snorted. "Sure, sure. Let me get the food we ordered first, though, and notify my fiancé where we are."

"Of course, sir."

On second thought.... "Actually, there is something I need help with. I had to acquisition a schooner to get up here, see, and..."

Our passenger ship was nothing like the little schooner that had sailed us around half of Chahir. At a whopping 440 feet in length, with a full five-mast rig, it made the schooner look like a glorified rowboat. In a way, it was. Aletha had done well in booking us on this ship, though. With her charm and wit, she'd managed to land us the honeymoon cabin, and so we had more space on board than a normal cabin would've given us. For a ship cabin, it was actually comfortable. Around the size of an inn room, with a bathroom of sorts attached. (I still had to stand sideways and walk like a crab to maneuver in the bathroom, but at least I *could* move around in it.)

This cabin had a connecting door to Becca's cabin, too, which put most of my paranoid instincts to rest. If something did happen in the middle of the night, I could be there in a second.

I'd barely managed to get a good look at the room when a cabin boy rapped on the open door and said, "Pardon, sir, but Captain requests an audience with you and your family."

Oh? I wondered what this was about. I hoped it wasn't because a certain Jaunten horse was refusing to board. We'd had a loooong talk about that this morning before coming over here. "A moment."

I went through the connecting door and said, "Captain wants a word with us."

Aletha paused in opening Becca's traveling case. "About?"

"That is the extent of my knowledge."

Eyebrow quirked, she gestured me back out.

We followed the cabin boy down the hallway and up a short flight of stairs before the cabin boy knocked on a rather impressive wooden door. When he heard a call from inside, he simply shoved it inwards and announced, "Here they be, Captain."

"Thank you, Squid."

"Ma'am." Squid—surely that was a nickname?— bobbed his head at us before disappearing back the way he'd come.

"I'm Kayla Kawajan," she greeted us through the open door. "Captain of the *Northern Star*. Come in, come in." Captain Kayla Kawajan was a round woman, in face and body, with hair stuck up in a permanent braid around her head and a ready smile. She gave off the feeling of liking everyone and everything, until someone crossed her, and then she would become as ruthless as an upset dragon. I'd met captains like her before and recognized the type well. Needless to say, her passengers would adore her, and her crew have a healthy fear of her.

She pulled the three of us into her office and welcomed us with a smile. "Please, sit," she invited in a husky voice. "There's a few things we need to cover before I marry you two."

I couldn't begin to think of what. Aletha had assured me she'd taken care of the paperwork and had already registered our marriage before we boarded ship. But I sat in the chair she pointed to regardless, making way for Becca as I did. And then making more space for Tail, as wherever Becca sat, Tail would too.

As we got comfortable, I took a better look at my surroundings. Strangely, it didn't fit with my idea of a ship's office. I expected elaborate woodcarvings in the beams, and painted gold gilding the edges. Instead, the simple desk, four chairs, and the landscape hanging on the wall could belong in any earthbound office. The only thing that looked different was the bay windows behind the desk, which looked out over the ocean. Well, that and the fact that all of the furniture was bolted to the floor.

When we settled, the captain put her back to the edge of the desk and leaned against it, facing us square-on. "I couldn't help but notice *who* I'm marrying today. Captain Riicshaden, Second Lieutenant Aletha Saboton, it's an honor to meet you. I've heard a great deal through rumors and such, so I have a good notion of who you are."

Oh. I shared a quick glance with Aletha. We hadn't expected that a ship captain would recognize us, but that was silly in hindsight. This woman traveled up and down the coast and probably heard more rumors in a year than I would in a lifetime.

"Because I know who you are," she continued, "I have to ask—are you sure you want to be married this way? People of your notoriety would surely warrant a grander ceremony."

"It's the grand ceremony we're trying to avoid," Aletha admitted. "Neither of us cares much for that."

Her grey eyes looked the both of us over carefully, then she smiled. "As long as you've thought it through. I certainly would like to boast that I married you. Then, to the other matter. About the vows."

It abruptly occurred to me that I was repeating what Garth had done. I was marrying a woman of a different nationality, and of *course* they would have their own notion of what 'proper vows' would be.

Aletha realized it in the same moment and snapped her fingers. "I forgot. Chahiran vows are different."

"And if you don't use those vows with a Chahiran, you're not legally married in Chahir," Captain Kawajan said firmly. "Which is why I must ask, where do you plan to live after you're married? Your answer will determine which vows I can use."

"Isle of Strae," I admitted.

"Strae Academy, to be precise," Aletha amended.

Kawajan's eyebrows rose. "Strae Academy?"

"I'm the Weapons Professor there, you see," I explained. "And the little girl in my lap is not only my sister, but a young mage."

Kawajan focused on Becca for the first time. "Is that right? Then it's an honor to meet you as well,

Magess."

Becca gave her a shy smile.

"So, you're bound for the Isle of Strae, eh? Well, in that case, I think our course is clear. We must use the Chahiran set of vows, otherwise you won't be legally wed." Kawajan nodded, content with her own conclusion. "In that case, there's a few things I need to tidy up and such before we marry you off. I do want to explain, though, that we have a long tradition on this ship where marriages are concerned. You see, we've always had the wedding in the main dining hall, with my crew in their best dress. Once you exchange vows and rings, then you're seated with me at the head table, and everyone is given the chance to toast you if they wish to. After that, we just have a grand time partying."

Now, *that* sounded like an ideal wedding ceremony to me. No real fuss. After hearing Becca and Aletha talk about weddings for days on end, though, I knew better than to say anything before knowing what Aletha thought of this. I turned to ask, but the smile on her face was answer enough. "Gorgeous, I take it this is perfect?"

"Perfect," she agreed, smile stretching from ear to ear.

"I'm not familiar with the Solian vows, but I'm willing to use them if you want to teach them to me," Kawajan offered to her. "We can just do double vows, cover all the stops."

"There actually *isn't* a standard wedding vow for Sol," Aletha responded with a wry shrug. "Each city-state has its own version. As long as it's properly registered with your city-state, they're fine. I will need a second copy of the marriage license to give to Ascalon."

Kawajan nodded. "That's easily done. Then, one last thing. How do you want your new married name to read?"

Aletha blinked at her. Then blinked again. "Oh, great guardians, my name will be Chahiran after this!"

I threw back my head and laughed out loud. "You honestly didn't think about that?"

She shot me a dirty look. "When, in the past three days, have I had time to think about it?"

"But seriously," I insisted, "after all that trouble that Chatta went through to figure out how to work her name into the Chahiran naming system, it didn't occur to you at all?"

"No," she groused, looking peeved. "But it should have. Captain Kawajan, have you been in this situation before? Marrying people of different nationalities I mean."

"Often," the captain responded easily. "People think it's romantic to elope and get married at sea, for some reason. Normally ends up with one or the other seasick the entire trip, which doesn't make for much of a honeymoon, in my opinion."

"So what have you seen? When people try to merge their maiden name with their married one."

"Oh, all sorts of varieties. I've seen one woman hyphenate it, where they use their husband's family name, hyphen, and then their maiden name. I've seen where the woman just takes her first name and inserts it into the Chahiran name. I've seen where she put the family name first, then her maiden name, then her first name—turns into a mouthful, that does."

"Chatta's first name alone was a mouthful," I recalled. "That's why she stuck with her nickname instead."

"Riic-Saboton Aletha?" Aletha tried out dubiously, mouth pursing. "Riicsabotonalethaan? Guardians, no, it sounds like a disease."

Becca must have agreed, as she giggled. "Rii-calethaan," she suggested.

Aletha gave a solemn nod. "Only one that makes sense to me. At least I can say it without turning my tongue into knots."

"I'll put Riicalethaan on the license, then." Kawa-jan clapped her hands together, the sound unreasonably loud. "Dinner's served sharply at six. I'll meet you at the doors."

The captain—an astute woman—had charitably given us the cabin right next door for Becca and Tail at half-price. At first I wanted to refuse it, but she explained that it was something of a wedding gift. I, for one, was grateful to her as it helped lower the cost of the trip.

It might have been unwise to book a separate

cabin to begin with, but I didn't want to spend my wedding night with a little girl and a furball wedged in between me and my bride.

We more or less would have emptied our pockets paying for all of this if not for our run-in with the city guard the day before. They'd refilled my wallet after I'd told them the full tale of our journey. I hadn't tried to stop them, either.

Little girls were *expensive*.

Wives weren't much better!

I was unpacking our bags into the chest at the foot of the bed when Aletha stuck her head inside the room and informed me, "Your horse is refusing to board."

Turning, I gave her a dismayed look. "What, they're still loading the horses?"

"Just yours, darling."

Remind me again why I wanted a sentient mount? "Right," I sighed. "I'm coming."

"Coming with an idea of how to convince him to board, I hope," Aletha responded, leading the way through the narrow hallways. "Unlike Night, he cannot be bribed with peanut butter."

"I'm fresh out of ideas and open to suggestions."

Becca appeared in the hallway. "Tail said he'd talk to him."

It took a second for that sentence to make sense. When it did, I had to bite my lip to keep my humor in check. A cat was going to talk sense into a horse? Now I had to see this. "Is that right? Lead on, then."

We trooped back down to the dock level, where a certain white horse stood in front of a gangplank.

Cloud had all four hooves planted, a stubborn look in his eye, and his head held up high, refusing to let anyone touch his halter. When he saw us, he paused and lowered his head a little. Was it my imagination, or did he look nervous?

Tail leaped lightly out of Becca's arms and strode toward the stallion. He stopped right in front of Cloud, one paw clawing the air as if to say, 'Get your head down here, I can't talk to you like this.'

I noticed as we stood off to the side that other people were taking notice of this odd pairing and were gathering around, at first in unobtrusive ways, then in more obvious ones.

Cloud hesitated, but he finally lowered his head so that he was more on an eye level with Tail.

Now, I didn't speak cat. I didn't speak horse, either. But I swear to you that a severe tongue-lashing happened right in front of my eyes. Tail's ears were flat against his head, fur rising along his spine, and if he'd still possessed a tail, it would have been lashing.

Cloud hunched in place, looking hangdog, but he really didn't want to board the ship, in spite of everything Tail was saying. He whinnied in a plaintive way and tossed his head.

Tail growled in warning.

"Now, Tail, don't be mean." Becca left my side and went to Cloud, where she put a hand on his nose and stroked it soothingly. "Cloud, I know you don't want to go on a ship again. But this is a bigger ship, it won't be so cramped, and you'll have other horses to talk to."

Cloud failed to be moved.

Pursing her lips, she tried again. "You want to be a Nreesce, don't you?"

The horse visibly hesitated.

From the side of her mouth, Aletha asked me, "Did you tell her he could become a Nreesce?"

I was just as confused. "No. I wonder where she..." I paused as a conversation from several nights ago came back to me. "I did tell her about Life Mages, though. And there's some at Strae."

"Ahhh, and she put the pieces together. And at some point, talked to Cloud about it. Well, within the realms of magic, making him a full Nreesce is totally possible. Or at least I think it is."

"I'm sure it is," I responded absently, eyes still trained on the trio arguing it out. "Cloud should be sure of this, too. After all, Nreesces were created from normal horses in the very beginning."

"Advent Eve's knowledge telling you that?"

"You gotta love being Jaunten sometimes."

I missed something, as Becca had gotten a response from Cloud, because she responded in exasperation, "Well, how do you expect to become one if you won't even go to the island?"

Tail, at her feet, growled something that just sounded derisive.

Becca scooted in a little closer, voice crooning, "I'll feed you peanut butter. Just like a real Nreesce would eat."

Cloud looked at her steadily, then at the boat, before giving a long sigh.

Beaming, she rubbed at his nose. "That's a good Cloud."

A handler from the ship (who looked bemused by this conversation), cautiously approached and tried to lead Cloud up the gangplank and into the ship again. This time, it worked.

Pleased with herself, Becca scooped up her cat and skipped back toward us. I swear, you'd mistake her for a Life Mage if you didn't know better. Since when did she know how to speak horse, anyway?

"What were you saying, Gorgeous, about peanut butter not working?"

"I stand corrected."

Our marriage that night was pleasantly simple and fun. Also nerve-wracking. At least for me it was. Aletha seemed perfectly at ease—excited, but hardly nervous. I think it was just me that had a momentary chill chase its way up my spine as I realized that I had not just one, but now *two* women that I'd sworn to see protected and happy. I'd fought in multiple battles, against opponents armed with everything from swords to magic, and helped to chase down and eliminate an entire magic order.

Keeping those two oaths would be much harder.

Still, I felt that working for a future with my two girls would be entirely worth it after I got a good look at them. Aletha was dressed in a stunning red dress, looking feminine in a way that I'd rarely seen her. In fact, the last time I recalled seeing her look that deliciously gorgeous was at Garth and Chatta's wedding.

Becca wore her new blue dress, her hair done up in ringlets, and she must have been a little too entranced by it, as she kept rising up on her toes and doing pirouettes.

Tail found a high beam to sit on and ignored us entirely.

The captain found us at the door, as promised, and led us to the front of the room where the head table was laid out with a banquet of food. In a loud voice, she announced our ceremony was beginning, then oversaw us as we exchanged vows and rings. I kissed my new wife (to much cheering and catcalling), and then we spent the rest of the night partying.

I regretted that the next morning. Did you know that you could be hung over from eating too much?

For the next four days of the journey, I adjusted to being an old married man. Strange, how I thought I knew this woman so well, and yet as a wife, I didn't know her at all. We were somewhat awkward around each other at first, trying to find our rhythm in this new partnership, but eventually we found our stride and settled tentatively into it.

Aletha and I both took turns sitting topside with Becca and working with her on her control. We encouraged her to use her magic here as she had on the schooner, speeding us along. In a massive ship like this, we wouldn't get near the speed we did last time, but we were sailing at a faster clip.

I think Captain Kawajan suspected we were up to something, as she often paused and watched these sessions with suspicious eyes. She didn't say anything to us, though. After all, a captain that made it to port early got a bonus. If I were her, I certainly wouldn't risk losing that bonus by prying.

Aletha and I didn't know much about magic, but our simple presence next to Becca as she worked her magic seemed to be a steadying force. After all this practice, she hardly felt nervous anymore, but she still didn't get far from us as she coaxed the winds to push us along. I often had the little girl and cat in my lap for hours at a time.

As I sat there with Becca, it reminded me of something from my own childhood. In fact, magic element aside, it strongly put me in mind of a nightly habit my father and I had.

One of my favorite memories with my father was lying out on the grass and stargazing with him. We didn't know much about the heavens, but it was a good chance for me to just connect with him. I knew that when we were out there, my mother wouldn't disturb us and I could ask him whatever question that came into my head. I asked him some pretty absurd things, too, but he always answered me.

It was only as an adult that I realized, half the time, he hadn't known the answer and was making things up out of hot air. Still, the answers hadn't been important most of the time. What *had* been important was that he listened to me and was willing to answer me.

I didn't know much about combing hair, or shopping, or any of those other things that girls do. But I'd like to think I knew a little about how to be a good father figure, considering I'd had a good role model.

So after dinner, I whispered my plan to Aletha, then snagged Becca and dragged her up to the foredeck, where we could have space and privacy.

"What are we doing?" Becca asked me as I sank onto the decking.

"Stargazing," I answered promptly.

That must have sounded suitably romantic, as she gave a pleased "Oh!" and plunked right down next to me.

We shifted and squirmed about until we were both flat on our backs and comfortable. I had an arm tucked under my head, and my other arm was being used by Becca for her pillow. She gazed up in silence for a long time. "They're pretty."

"They are," I agreed.

The waves lapped against the side of the ship, and a mild breeze drifted over us. It was a perfect night for stargazing, and I was suddenly proud of myself for thinking of it.

"Shad?" Becca wiggled about until she was propped up on my chest.

"Hmmm?"

"How did you become the best soldier ever?"

Now there was a question few had thought to ask me. They usually asked if I could teach someone else to be as good as I was. "Well, it's quite the story, sweetie."

Her jaw firmed in a mulish slant.

Not put-off by this, eh? I grinned at her. "Alright, from the beginning, then. I was rather young when the Magic War broke out. Just turning fourteen. I was in a fair-sized city at the time, and I saw more than one duel break out right in front of me. I watched them—

usually from a safe distance—battle it out with each other, and I realized that as dangerous as magic was, it took *time* to cast a spell. In fact, an archer can aim and release an arrow as fast as a magician can cast a curse. Watching them work, I had this crazy idea that I could run faster than they could cast, and beat them with sheer speed."

She blinked at me. "Could you?"

"Not at first." I laughed in memory. "But the first year you're training in swordsmanship, a *turtle* stands a good chance against you. Your muscles aren't used to the weight of the practice sword, much less a real broadsword. You're not quick enough to do anything. But the idea just wouldn't leave my mind. I was convinced that if only I practiced a little harder, a little longer than everyone else, I really could do it."

"So you did."

"Well, I cheated a little," I admitted. "I created arm and leg weights that I could strap on. I practiced with them, ate and slept and did everything with those weights on me. It was hard at first. I felt like I was in constant pain and dragging through every step. But eventually I got used to the weights."

"And you got faster?" she guessed, intrigued by this.

"And I got faster," I confirmed. "And then I made heavier weights."

She blinked, head jerking back a little. "What? Why?"

"Because I still wasn't fast enough. I put on heavier weights, and when I got used to those, I put on another set of heavier weights, and I kept doing that until I could keep up with any other swordsman even with the weights on. My master watched me do this, and didn't say a word for two years as I trained under him, but eventually he came to me and said, 'Well, boy, you're serious about this. I can see that. Might as well give you proper training.' I didn't know what he meant at first, but then he took me to a different training field and showed me. He'd fashioned an obstacle course specifically designed to challenge me and my so-called speed." I could still see it in my mind's eye, and my body remembered it clearly. "It had all sorts of things that I had to run around, jump over, dodge, and slice in order to make it through unscathed."

Becca looked at my face uncertainly. "Did you?"

"Not the first hundred times." I chuckled low and long. "I might have if he'd let me take my weights off, but of course he didn't. After that first hundred times, I got the hang of it. Then he changed the course and I ran it again another hundred times. I did that for three months straight before he finally let me take the weights off."

"And then you were fast enough?"

"And then I was fast enough." My eyes were looking up toward the heavens, but I didn't see the stars above me. "And then I was almost too fast. My body was so used to the weights that I felt like I was *flying* whenever I ran or fought. I had to get used to not having them on, and that took a good week. But after that, no magician stood a chance against me. I could fight them all, with just a sword in my hand, and subdue them. It was a blessing and a curse." Seeing that she didn't understand what I meant by that, I tried to explain. "You see, when you're *that* strong, where few people can fight you, it invites even worse trouble. I could protect a lot of people, true, but because I was so good, they sent me to the frontlines, to the worst parts of the battle. They knew I stood a better chance of facing off the magicians than anyone else, you see. And it was because I fought on the frontlines that I was injured so badly that they'd had no choice but to put me in a crystal and hope I survived."

"But it's a good thing you lived." She sounded so certain of that.

Well, to her, my backstory was a legend. One that she was privileged enough to hear from the man himself. She didn't understand the loss I felt when I realized how much time had passed and that my family was long since gone. It had been dark days. In fact, it'd taken me months to come to terms with it. If not for Xiaolang, and his quiet support, I wasn't sure I would have fared as well. The fact that I'd been given a ready mission to save Chahir had also helped tremendously. It'd given me something to do, a clear goal to achieve, instead of letting me stew in my grief. Thanks to my team, I'd been able to work through things and find a path in life again.

Of course, my chosen path had just taken a sharp turn, thanks to a certain Gardener with an agenda, but I didn't mind that, either. It was just an extension of saving Chahir, to my mind.

Aletha's dark head came up the stairs to where

she was just visible. "I hate to interrupt, but it's getting late."

Oh. Now, had she been hovering just out of sight, eavesdropping? I wouldn't put it past her. I took a better look at the moon and realized that she was right, it had gotten late. "Right, then. Off to bed we go."

I grabbed the girl and slung her over my shoulder like a barbarian carrying off spoils of war. She squealed and giggled as I tickled her behind the knees. (Note to self: that was a weak point, remember that.)

Aletha unfairly rescued her at Becca's cabin door and helped her get ready for bed. This involved a lot of giggling, for some reason. I was washed, dressed, and in bed before Aletha made it back to our cabin.

As I listened to my new wife putter about getting ready for bed, I fell into a light doze, which lasted until she climbed into bed next to me. It let a mean draft of cool air in under the covers, which she made up for by cuddling into my right side. Aletha snuggled in close, head on my shoulder and whispered softly, "Do you regret it? That decision you made at fourteen."

So she *had* been listening. Well, she was a consummate sneak, after all.

I pondered her question for a moment, turning it over in my mind. "No," I decided at last. "I really can't regret it. Because it was my speed, my ability to fight when no one else could, that saved my family and friends from danger. I can't even unwish being stuck in that thrice-cursed crystal for two hundred years. I can't unwish you."

She tilted enough to press a kiss against my jaw.

"Thank you, darling."

I smiled and squeezed her a little tighter. She might take the words as flattery, but I meant it.

For a long moment, we just lay there, enjoying each other's company. Aletha broke the comfortable silence by asking suddenly, "Have you ever thought that maybe you were meant to be in this time?"

Giving my brain a second to turn that over didn't do an ounce of good. I still didn't understand what she was driving at. "Come again?"

"Garth often said that ley line or not, he couldn't understand why the healing spells on the crystal lasted as long as they did. They really should have run out, or worn down, decades before. When he said that the first time, I didn't pay much attention, but later on, I wondered. We've seen the Gardeners have a direct hand in people's lives before, meddling when they deem a person necessary. Don't you wonder if they did that with you?"

It was on the tip of my tongue to tell her she was being silly, that there was no way that could be the case, and yet the words wouldn't come.

We knew from the records that the Weather Mages had disappeared more or less five months before I was sealed into the crystal.

The Gardeners would know that the magical line had ended, and it would likely take some time to bring it back, as the condition of the land was directly under their care.

They knew it would take an Earth Mage to get me out of that crystal.

They knew that it would take years, if not decades, for Chahir to be able to accept magic again.

They had to have known that there would be many magicians, and precious magical bloodlines, that would be at risk when magic was revived.

And who had they called when those dangers became apparent?

Me.

"Shad. Breathe."

I had to remind myself I knew how to do that.

Aletha popped her head up to look at my face. "Guardians. You think I'm right."

"I think your question hits a little too close to home, yes," I managed around a dry mouth. "Considering that it was a Gardener that came and gave me the task, do you really think it's such a stretch that they would *preserve* me for that task?"

Her mouth formed a soundless 'oh.' "I hadn't thought of it like that...." she trailed off, eyes going blind.

My sense of humor kicked in. "Well, thank you, darling wife, for that disturbing insight. If you don't mind, I'll lie awake the next few nights thinking about it."

It took her a second, but then she grinned back at me, crookedly. "You're welcome?"

"Just when I think life can't get any stranger...." I shook my head minutely.

"You think being stuck in a magical crystal is strange?" she asked in feigned shock.

I snorted. "Not to mention being turned Jaunten

by a horse."

"Or you turning a cat and another horse Jaunten?" she retaliated archly.

"Or being married to a woman that's two hundred years younger than I am?"

Aletha choked. "Great guardians, you're right!"

I cackled because I'd made her flinch first.

She poked me in the ribs for that one, hard. "You're awful. Remind me, why did I marry you, again?"

"For the free entertainment."

A piercing scream rent the air in two.

I was up, out of the bed, and with sword in hand before I could even get my eyes fully open. In sheer instinct, I slammed open the connecting door, eyes darting around the room, looking for the enemy.

Only I didn't see one.

Becca was up on the chest at the end of the bed, still screaming, pointing to the far corner of the room. "Kill it!" she demanded, voice rising in octave. "Someone kill it!"

Aletha came in right behind me, her sword also in hand. "What?" she demanded.

"There's a mouse!"

Huh? A mouse? I sank onto my haunches and tilted my head, getting a better look. Oh, sure enough, there was one hunkered into the corner over there. Little bit of a thing, I doubted it was full-grown yet. I wasn't sure who was more scared, girl or mouse. "Becca, calm down, it's nowhere near you—"

Not getting the reaction she wanted (although, really, what did she expect me to do, axe the thing with my sword?) she wisely turned to Tail next. "I want it *dead*," she snarled.

Tail gave the most pleased, feline grin I'd ever seen on him. Then he dove off the bed and straight for the mouse.

Poor little thing squeaked in terror, running around in circles, trying to find an exit. There wasn't one.

Needless to say, it didn't last long.

Tail hopped onto the windowsill, pushing the latch open, and neatly dumped the carcass into the sea before turning back around, completely dignified.

Only then did Becca relax. A smidgen, that was. She gave me a look that borderlined terror. "Shad, are there more?"

"Probably?" I offered, rubbing at the back of my head. "Rats and mice are common on ships like this, Becca. They follow the food stores that are loaded on board, you see. And then they travel up the ropes to get on the ship."

Not the answer she wanted to hear, judging by that mulish set to her jaw. "Tail. Kill them *all*."

Bloodthirsty little thing, wasn't she?

I did believe that order made Tail's day. Human intelligence or not, he still had a cat's instincts, I guess. With a purr, he bounced to the floor and took off through our feet, heading for the main part of the ship.

One could almost feel sorry for the mice.

Tail spent the next few days happily chasing mice around the ship and disposing of them overboard. Most of the passengers, having found mice in places they'd rather not have rodents, cheered him on. Becca rewarded him handsomely every night for his labors of the day, usually in some form of fishy delicacy.

In retrospect, I really should have predicted what happened next.

Squid came and found me just before dinner one night, about four days into Tail's mouse-hunting, with a flushed face and a worried look in his eye. "Sir, that white cat's yours, ain't it?"

"My sister's, yes. Why?" I was struck by a sudden sense of foreboding.

"Come quick, sir! He's been found in the kitchen, and the head chef's threatenin' to chop his ears off to match his missing tail."

Now there was a mental picture for you. I knew where the kitchen was at this point and didn't need a guide, so I pushed past him and ran as fast as I could through the narrow, cramped confines of the hallways until I skidded to a stop in front of the kitchen door.

The place was a madhouse—it normally was, trying to feed a boat full of hungry people—with a dozen men weaving their way in and around each other, metal pots clanging, knives flashing, and a wave of heat and spices hitting me directly in the face as I strode through the door.

A commotion in the very back corner of the room caught my attention, and I made a beeline for it, dodging men with hot pots and knives as I went.

Tail was underneath a counter, lying nearly flat to the floor, growling in the back of his throat. A portly man with ruddy cheeks and a bloodstained apron stood in front of him, brandishing cleavers in both hands. "You get out of my kitchen, you filthy beast!" the man was yelling, his Hainish accent so thick that he was barely understandable. "OUT!"

I caught one of his wrists, and his head snapped around to stare at me.

Assured he wouldn't be waving that cleaver around in an area I didn't want, I bent enough to meet Tail's eyes. "Paw caught in the cookie jar, Tail?"

Tail gave me a disgusted look, another growl coming from him.

Wagging my finger at him, I tsked him. "If you participate in my jokes, I will participate in your rescue."

At that, he rolled his eyes.

"Is that infernal beast yours?!" the man bellowed.

"Not precisely. My sister's, and the reason he's here is he was chasing after a mouse." I looked at him pointedly.

The man, if possible, became redder in the face. "A mouse! A RODENT IN MY KITCHEN? Intolerable!"

"I agree, completely," I managed with an outraged tone of my own. "Now, if you want to chase after the mouse with those cleavers, be my guest, but if I were you, I'd leave it up to him. He's better equipped for mouse-hunting than either of us."

The chef hesitated. "But...a cat in my kitchen...."

"He won't go near the food or trip anyone up," I soothed him. "A very smart cat, this one. Why, he's been helping the passengers get mice out of their cabins for days now."

"Days, you say? Then the captain knows about this?"

Surely she did by now. I mean, it'd been the talk at dinner for the past two nights, at least. "Of course she does!" I assured him, releasing the cleaver to give him a hearty clap on the back.

"Well," he lowered the cleaver, still looking at Tail suspiciously, "if he has the captain's approval, then..."

"Splendid!" It wasn't a lie. Just a campaign in misinformation. "Tail, do continue with your hard work."

If Tail could speak in the human language, I'm fairly certain he would have cussed us both out at that point. As it was, I hardly got any thanks or gratitude for my assistance. Instead, he crawled out from underneath the counter and bounded away, heading for the direction the mouse must have disappeared to. Either that, or he just chose to get out of range of those cleavers while he could.

Me? I chose to get out of the kitchen as well, before the chef had the notion to ask more questions.

The *Northern Star* made a record time of twelve days to reach Greathouse Harbor. Becca's cheating with the wind had much to do with that. No one was complaining about a shortened trip. We were all rather tired of being on board after the ninth day.

The ship creaked and tilted ever so slightly as the captain turned her, heading toward the docks. The harbor, of course, was the one that faced the Isle of Strae. As we came into dock, I stood with Becca at the railing, wanting to point out our new home. "Do you see it?"

She lifted a hand to shield her eyes from the sun and squinted. "Is it a castle?"

"Rather looks like one, eh? But it's far larger than any castle I've seen. Almost the size of a palace, that thing is."

"Shad..." She leaned forward more, trying to see better. "The water looks funny around it."

"Your eyes aren't playing tricks on you, kiddo," I assured her with a laugh. "The water really isn't touching the island."

Her eyes crossed. "Magic can do that?!"

"You'll be amazed what magic can do." I leaned against the railing so we were more on the same level. "Garth had it designed that way to protect the students there. He said it would require being accompanied by another magician to arrive on the Isle, which would prevent people from just showing up when they wanted to."

"Oh." Becca chewed on that for a moment. "But I don't know how to get us there."

I patted her head. "Don't worry, I never expected you to do anything. We'll call Garth when we get to the harbor and ask him to come get us." Assuming he didn't have someone standing by waiting on us. He might. Depended on how short on manpower he was.

She'd been aiming to reach this place for weeks now, but with it sitting there right in front of her eyes, I didn't think she knew how to feel about finally reaching the destination.

I pulled her into my side with an arm around her shoulders. "It'll be fine, lovey. You're going to a place of magic and wonder. There's talking horses, flying cats that can pick any lock, witches and wizards and other mages like you."

Becca gave me a funny look. "Tail won't be the only cat there?"

Had I not mentioned the Meurittas before? I snorted. "Not by a long shot."

From the main deck, I heard a familiar captain's voice boom out, "THANK YOU, PASSENGERS, FOR RIDING THE *NORTHERN STAR*. PLEASE PREPARE TO DISEMBARK!"

"That sounds like our cue, kiddo." I stepped away and gave her a gamine grin. "Ready for the next adventure?"

She grabbed one of my hands with both of hers, still looking a little unsure about all of this. "You'll stay with me?"

"Every step of the way."

Aletha and I divided up duties. I took the girl and her cat with me to the nearest relay station to call Garth. She grabbed our horses and gear and went to the designated dock for Strae-bound pedestrians.

And it would be pedestrians. One could hardly climb in a boat to reach that isle, after all.

Becca and I had to wander around the docks a bit and ask several people, but eventually we got good directions. In fact, the place we wanted was only two blocks away. I noted their close proximity and wondered, was Garth's hand in that? It would certainly make it easier for people trying to get to Strae to call for help that way.

I definitely appreciated its closeness.

Having learned my lesson, I kept a tight grip on Becca's hand as we walked the streets, Tail following us like a white shadow. The directions we'd gotten from the dockhand were spot-on and I navigated my way there like I knew where I was going.

I walked into the office with an inner sense of relief. All I had to do was call Garth—or Chatta, I didn't really care—and have them come get us, and this nightmare of a trip would be over. Well, mostly over. Aletha and I still had to sort out the Ascalon situation, and move everything to Strae, but we'd have plenty of help doing all of that.

This relay office looked like every other one of its kind. A simple building, with one room, divided in half by a counter for the patrons with a bored young magician sitting behind it. He looked to be fifteen or so, in black robes, and I just knew he was here serving out an internship. He perked up slightly as I stepped through, then his eyes took in the young girl walking primly beside me and his jaw nearly dented the floor.

Oh brother. I snapped my fingers in front of his nose. "Yes, she's a Weather Mage. Focus for a moment, I need your help."

"*That's* what she is?" he squeaked in amazement. Hadn't quite passed out of puberty entirely, eh?

"Yes," Becca informed him seriously. She was studying him just as curiously. "You glow white. What does that mean?"

"H-huh?" He had to shake his head a little to pull himself together. "Oh, I'm a wizard. Masseryanen is my name."

Becca bobbed her head at him. "Riicbeccaan, pleasure to exchange names. This is Tail."

"Ahhhh…" He hopped lightly off his barstool and leaned over the counter to see what she was pointing at. When he did get a proper look, his eyes crossed. "Is…that possibly…"

"A Jaunten cat," I assured him, enjoying his reactions. These surprised questions never got old. "Now, Ryan, focus. I need to send a message to Strae. By mirror, if possible."

"Oh! Certainly, sir." He still lingered at the counter, although he couldn't seem to decide which he wanted to stare at more, Becca or Tail. Finally, he managed to get a mirror out of the drawer beside him and set it on the counter, where he then tilted it so that he could activate it, but I could speak into it. "Who should I call for you?"

"Garth," I answered.

That made Ryan pause, and he looked at me, truly *looked,* as if seeing me for the first time. It was obvious when everything clicked and he had an idea of who I was. He swallowed, hard, and his voice went back to squeaking. "Ah, yes, sir." Clutching the mirror tightly, he cleared his throat once, then again, before saying unsteadily, "Garth. Ah, that is, Magus Rheben-garthen?"

There were a few clicks, as if a woman in high heels approached, then the mirror spoke in a very familiar tone. "*He isn't in at the moment. This is Rhe-benchattaan.*"

"Beautiful," I greeted.

"*Shad!*" Chatta exclaimed, a mix of delight and relief in her tone. "*You rascal, that note you sent us left much to be desired. I'll skin you for that.*"

I tsked her, chuckling. "Now, now, cryptic notes are always more fun. It leaves you guessing what I meant."

"*That's exactly what's unfun about them. Where are you? Are you alright?*"

"Everyone's fine, and we're at Greathouse Harbor. Any chance you can run your husband down and ask him to come fetch us?"

"*You're already here?!*" she exclaimed. "*Heavens, you made good time!*"

I decided to explain later how Becca had cheated

and thereby set a new speed record for the *Northern Star*. "Yes, we did."

"*Wait, I'll find him. He's actually in the gardens, so it shouldn't take more than a minute. Can you wait for him by the landing dock?*"

"On our way," I assured her. "Oh, and Chatta?"

"*Yes?*"

"One thing, the position for Weapons Professor, can that be a dual position?"

"*I certainly think it's a two-man job, if that's what you're asking.*"

"No, more like I was wondering if you'd hire one more person to work alongside me."

"*If you know someone that will take the job, I certainly will!*"

"Actually, my wife said she would."

There was a very pregnant pause. "*Shad.*"

I grinned in anticipation. "Yes, Beautiful."

"*Are you telling me that you're married?*"

"Yes, I am."

Another long, pregnant moment of silence. "*To whom?*"

"Gorgeous."

Chatta spluttered over that one for a few moments. "*Since when were the two of you married?!*"

"As of about...two weeks ago."

"*You two GOT MARRIED WITHOUT YOUR FRIENDS IN ATTENDANCE?!*"

"Didn't want an elaborate ceremony," I explained, trying not to laugh. Chatta had the best reactions. "You're welcome to throw a party or a reception or something for us though."

"*Shad*," she gritted out through clenched teeth, "*you're telling me this NOW? You have the worst sense of timing!*"

"I have perfect timing," I corrected her jovially. "You can't hex me from there."

"*Oooh, you just wait until I get my hands on you!*"

"Now, Beautiful, calm down. You wouldn't want to make your dear friend a widow already, would you?"

"*I'm pretty sure at this point I'd be doing her a favor!*"

As I was half-convinced Aletha was crazy to marry me to begin with, I couldn't disagree with Chatta. "Well, you'll get your chance at it soon enough. See you soon!"

Chatta must have found her husband and filled him in with record speed, as Becca and I barely had time to rejoin Aletha before we saw him on the isle building his bridge.

Aletha greeted us by saying, "You must have reached him quickly. He just started on the bridge a moment ago."

"Reached Beautiful, actually," I corrected, coming to stand alongside her. The first time I'd been here, this dock was nothing more than a plain wooden structure jutting out over the water. But since then, someone (I bet I knew who) had rebuilt it into a sturdy dock of granite, all of it locked together so neatly that it didn't even need mortar to hold it place. It had quite a width to it, too, as if capable of holding several wagons at once.

"Chatta? What did she say?"

"That she'd skin me as soon as she saw me," I responded, not worried.

Aletha laughed. "You must have told her we're

married."

"For some strange reason, she's not mad at *you.*
Just me. Care to explain that?"

"Women's logic."

I pondered that for a moment. "Not helpful, dearest."

She shrugged, not bothered by this, eyes still sparkling with laughter.

Becca was still hanging onto my hand, and she
leaned her body weight forward, trusting me to keep
her from face-planting. "He's building that *really*
fast," she observed in admiration.

Yes he was. I expected Garth to be here within
the next two minutes, as he was walking along the
bridge even as he built it. The distance between here
and there wasn't much, and the stone seemed to melt
and flow under his magical direction, forming into a
flat bridge a good two hundred feet across. Despite
the fact that it was suspended over thin air, it looked
perfectly solid and safe to travel on.

We patiently watched his calm, unhurried approach. Garth stepped off his bridge with easy flair, as
if he was accustomed to walking on things that had no
support struts or pillars to sustain it. But then, I wanted to see the stone that would dare disobey an Earth
Mage. Showing that his Hainian wife had corrupted
him, he didn't greet us as a Chahiran would, but with
ready hugs.

"Aletha."

Aletha grinned and freely returned the embrace.
"Garth. You look well!"

"And all of you are in one piece, which I'm relieved to see." He stepped back, smile going lopsided. "You realize that as soon as you're at Strae, Chatta's going to give you an earful."

"Oh, I have my sacrificial goat handy," she assured him.

Ummm. She didn't mean me, did she? No, of course she did.

Chuckling, Garth turned to me and extended a hand, which I firmly clasped. "Shad. Only you can go on a dangerous mission and *still* manage to make mischief in the process."

"Isn't Residential Mischief Maker my job?" I asked, trying to look confused.

"You *can* take a break from that occupation now and again," he responded dryly. "We won't mind, promise. Now." Garth sank down to one knee, a gentle smile on his face and obvious relief in his eyes. He didn't need me or anyone else to tell him he was facing a Weather Mage. His magical senses must've been screaming at him. "I'm Rhebengarthen, an Earth Mage," he introduced himself.

"This is Riicbeccaan," I introduced her.

Garth gave me a confused look at the surname, but he inclined his head toward her. "Welcome, young Weather Mage."

Becca's eyes were as round as saucers, and I think she forgot to breathe for a few moments as she stared fixedly at Garth. "You...you *glow.*"

"Brown and green?" he returned, eyes softening. "Yes, I know."

"No, you *glow*," she repeated, emphasizing the word and attaching a significance to it. "You're the Balancer."

...What did she just say?

Garth's eyes narrowed slightly. "I was that, yes. How do you know?"

"The Gardener said the Guardian would take me to the Balancer," she answered simply, still staring at him in awe.

Garth about swallowed his tongue. "You...met a Gardener?"

She nodded absently. "The Gardener said you're supposed to teach me. He said it would be my task next, and you'd know what I'd need to do. That part I didn't understand," she confessed.

He had to swallow hard before he could croak, "It means, my dear, that you will be the next Balancer of this world."

"But I'm little!" Becca protested instinctively. She half-flinched from him, as if tempted to hide behind me.

"I understand your panic, trust me," Garth responded wryly. "I felt the same. But Becca, the Gardeners never give us a task that we cannot accomplish. They know very well what we are capable of, you see. My job was to fix Chahir, influence it so that it would accept magic again. *Your* job is going to be to fix the land itself, give it enough rainfall to where it becomes green and lush like it used to be."

Becca's head shook almost continuously. "I don't know what that looks like!"

"Your Guardian does." Garth shot me a quick smile. "After all, he was alive during that time. He *remembers* what Chahir was like."

That stopped Becca's head shaking, and she paused, looking up at me. "Oh. You do?"

"I do," I assured her, stroking her hair. "In fact, I was the only one that remembered we were supposed to have Weather Mages. That might be why the Gardeners sent me for you."

I had no doubt she would think about this more later, but her eyes kept being drawn back to Garth, as a magnet to steel. Part of it was because she understood exactly who this man was. The Gardeners would have given her a very strong impression of him. But as I looked at him, I saw him with new eyes. In the past year, Garth had grown into his roles. He didn't look nervous or somewhat lost anymore. Even kneeling on the ground, eye to eye with another mage, he seemed to quietly radiate power and authority.

Garth extended a hand to her. "Won't you come with me, Becca? I promise to guide you as much as I can, teach you everything I know. The only danger you'll face in Strae will be from Shad's pranks."

I chuckled and didn't deny it.

Becca tentatively took his hand. "Tail can come too?"

Garth regarded the feline sitting patiently at her feet. "He certainly can. In fact, I insist upon it. While we cross the bridge, maybe you can tell me how you came to have a Jaunten cat as your familiar?"

She lowered her voice to a loud whisper. "Shad

did it."

Garth shot me a dry look. "Now, how did I know that would be the answer? I suppose the Jaunten horse behind you is your doing as well?"

I shrugged unrepentantly. "Whoops?"

Shaking his head, Garth regained his feet in an easy, smooth motion. "I truly want the full tale now. But that can wait until we are settled in, I think. Well, Professor, Professora, Magess, and Master Tail, shall we go to Strae Academy?"

About the Author

Over thirty years ago, in the hills of Tennessee, a nice, unsuspecting young couple had their first child. Their home has since then been slowly turned into a library as their daughter consistently brought books home over the years.

No one was surprised when she grew up, went to college, and got her Bachelor's in English. Despite the fact that she has a degree, and looks like a mature young woman, she's never grown out of her love for dragons, fairies and other fantastical creatures. With school done, she's ready to start her career, hopefully by blending two of her loves: books and fantasy.

Her website can be found here:
http://www.honorraconteur.com
or if you wish to speak directly with the author,
visit her forum at:
http://z13.invisionfree.com/adventmage/

Don't Miss These Other Fantastic Adventures!

Kingslayer
Honor Raconteur
$9.99

The Child Prince
Book One of the
Artifactor
$9.99